Jessica Darling's

★ IT ★

LIST 2

THE (totally not) GUARANTEED GUIDE to FRIENDS, FOES & FAUX FRIENDS

A NOVEL BY MEGAN MCCAFFERTY

poppy

LITTLE, BROWN AND COMPANY
New York   Boston

Poppy

Hachette Book Group
1290 Avenue of the Americas, New York, NY 10104
Visit us at lb-kids.com

Poppy is an imprint of Little, Brown and Company.
The Poppy name and logo are trademarks of Hachette Book Group, Inc.

The publisher is not responsible for websites (or their content) that are not owned by the publisher.

First Paperback Edition: May 2015
First published in hardcover in September 2014 by Little, Brown and Company

Library of Congress Cataloging-in-Publication Data

McCafferty, Megan.
  The (totally not) guaranteed guide to friends, foes & faux friends : a novel / by Megan McCafferty. — First edition.
    pages cm. — (Jessica Darling's it list ; #2)
  "Poppy."
  Summary: "Twelve-year-old Jessica Darling receives another cryptic list from her older sister, Bethany. While hosting a slumber party and planning a Halloween costume, Jessica tries to navigate the seventh grade social scene, with mixed results"— Provided by publisher.
    ISBN 978-0-316-24504-3 (hc) — ISBN 978-0-316-24502-9 (ebook) — ISBN 978-0-316-24503-6 (pb) [1. Junior high schools—Fiction. 2. Schools—Fiction. 3. Popularity—Fiction. 4. Individuality—Fiction. 5. Sleepovers—Fiction. 6. Halloween—Fiction. 7. Sisters—Fiction. 8. Family life—Fiction.] I. Title.
  PZ7.M47833742Top 2014
  [Fic]—dc23

                                                                    2013039845

10 9 8 7 6 5 4 3 2 1

RRD-C

Printed in the United States of America

*For my friends on the third
floor of the Princeton
Public Library*

Chapter One

Is it impossible for old elementary-school friends and new junior-high friends to all get along as just, you know, *friends*?

Good or bad, that's what I'm about to find out.

Lately my friends have been stirring up more drama than I can handle. This is really saying something because my first month of seventh grade was a doozy. Let's see. I went out for the CHEER TEAM!!! and face-planted with a *SPLAT!* when I tried—and failed—to do a simple cartwheel. DRAMA. I nearly lost a finger making an ugly spoon in Woodshop—a class I'M NOT SUPPOSED TO BE IN taught by a singing giant straight out of Harry Potter. More DRAMA. And how could I forget the time I dressed up as Mighty the Seagull—the Official Pineville Junior

High School Mascot—and shook my red-white-and-blue-feathered booty in front of the entire school? Everyone thought I was a crazy chicken. Well, except a ginormous lovesick goose who mistook me for his new girlfriend and chased me all over the football field until I smashed beak-first into the goalpost.

DRAMA. DRAMA. And more DRAMA.

All of which could be traced back to the IT List my big sister gave me the day before the start of seventh grade.

My sister, Bethany, isn't exactly rocking her fifth year of college—um, especially since she failed all her classes and may not *technically* be a student anymore—but she ruled school when she was my age. She was always the center of attention and never had a shortage of friends and boyfriends. Her classmates considered her such an expert on all things awesome that they persuaded her to put that wisdom into writing "Bethany Darling's IT List: The Guaranteed Guide to Popularity, Prettiness & Perfection." No big sister was more qualified to share secrets of social success. And no little sister was less qualified to follow them.

And yet tonight at dinner when I happened to mention that I was having some issues with my friends—okay, I was ranting about how they were totally driving me crazy—Bethany casually let it slip that she had *another* IT List that could solve all my girl drama.

And I was like, "WAIT. WHAT? WHOA! I MUST HAVE THAT NEXT LIST!"

"You're *sure* you want it?" Bethany asked skeptically. "After what happened last time?"

Or, rather, after what *didn't* happen. Despite the "Guaranteed" promise in the title, I haven't become popular, pretty, or anywhere near perfect. From Bethany's point of view, I'd taken all the right advice in all the wrong directions.

I, however, saw it differently.

"Are you kidding?" I replied. "I want to see it *because* of what happened last time."

A slow smile spread across Bethany's face.

"Okay," she said assertively. "Let me get it. It's in my bedroom."

Bethany excused herself from the dining room, and I could hardly contain myself in her absence. See, here's the thing about DRAMA: As painful as it can be sometimes, it certainly makes life more interesting. When I think about what seventh grade would have been like without the first IT List, I get kind of drowsy, and the next thing I know I'm ZZZZZZZ.

In other words: BORING.

A BAZILLION MINUTES LATER, Bethany breezed back in with an envelope in her hand. The second IT List!

"Are you suuuure you're in?" she asked teasingly.

"I'm in!" I promised. "I'm *so* in."

"In *what*?" asked my parents in the way that only my parents can.

I hadn't even noticed that they had finished cleaning up in the kitchen and were lurking in the doorway. My mom and dad are expert lurkers.

"In…" I stammered. "In…um…"

My sister shot me a warning look. Bethany wants to keep the IT Lists just between us. Maybe she's waiting until I'm confidently perched at the tippy-top of the social ladder before taking credit as the mastermind behind my meteoric rise from Not to Hot. Perhaps she doesn't want our parents blaming her for any subsequent face-breaking visits to the nurse's office. Who knows what's happening underneath that mane of glossy blond hair? With a ten-year gap between us, Bethany and I have had few opportunities to bond over sister-to-sister stuff. I'm more than happy to comply with her rules if it means she won't go back to forgetting that I exist.

"She's in with the in crowd," my sister clarified for me. "The IT clique."

Mom's eyes lit up. Dad's eyebrows shot up.

"Really!" said Mom.

"Really?" asked Dad.

"Really," confirmed my sister.

I thought, *No, not really.*

Then I considered how I had two friends on the elite CHEER TEAM!!! and two more friends on the super-duper-exclusive Spirit Squad and thought again.

Well, sort of.

I've noticed the way other girls in our grade pass our lunch table and look at us with something like envy because we sit in a totally up-and-coming part of the cafeteria surrounded by Hots.

Maybe?

"If she isn't already," Bethany said as she handed over the envelope, "she will be."

Then she blew kisses at all of us, said her good-byes, and dashed out the door. Bethany loves dramatic entrances and exits. She excels at them.

"What did she give you, Jessie?"

Mom craned her neck to see for herself. I instinctively tucked the IT List into the pouch of my sweatshirt. I needed to be as overprotective as a mama kangaroo.

"I don't know," I lied. "I haven't opened it yet. Duh."

My mother pinched her lips, torn between coming down on me for being rude and kissing up to me to find out what was in the envelope. Curiosity won out.

"Well," she said with a slightly strained expression,

"don't you want to know what's inside? Aren't you going to open it?"

Of course I wanted to know what was inside. *Obviously,* I was going to open it. I was dying to read the IT List, but I make a point of never looking too eager about anything in front of my parents because they'd instantly get all suspicious that I'm up to something shady. Then they'd start asking ridiculous questions I don't want to answer that would inevitably put a damper if not a major delay on the very thing I'm excited about. So I had to pretend not to care too much about Bethany's envelope if I ever hoped to read it in all its wisdom tonight.

"Eh. It's probably nothing." I nonchalantly pulled the drawstring on my hoodie. "I'll open it later."

My strategy worked. Before long the intrigue of the envelope faded, and the Darling household was restored to its normal state of boringness.

"Have you finished your homework?" Mom asked.

"Have you *started* your homework?" Dad asked.

Woo-hoo! It was the out I'd been waiting for.

"No and no," I blurted. "Gotta go hit the books!"

I hung a DO NOT DISTURB. HOMEWORK IN PROGRESS sign on my bedroom door. I'm usually a very diligent student. I always get my homework done before I watch TV or gossip with my friends. However, Language Arts and Pre-

Algebra were not my priorities just then. After all, I already knew the difference between a preposition and a participle, a matrix and a mode. But could I make it through one more day of lunch-table drama without the IT List? No, only the IT List contained the life-changing advice I really needed to learn if I was going to survive junior high with friends by my side.

Or so I hoped.

Chapter Two

IT List 2
The Guaranteed Guide to Friends,
Foes & Faux Friends

1. 1 BFF < 2 BFFs < 4 BFFs < 8 BFFs < INFINITY BFFs
2. Have fun with your enemies.
3. PARTY!!!
4. When all else fails: CANDY.
5. There is no I in CLIQUE.

That's it.

That's *IT*?

The document containing the secrets to a lifetime of stress-free friendships was written on the back of a glittery invitation to a slumber party that took place at the house of some girl named Julia almost ten years ago. That might sound strange, but the first IT List had been written in lip liner on the back of a ten-year-old Pineville Junior High CHEER TEAM!!! travel schedule.

And like its predecessor, IT List 2 left me with more questions than answers.

As they came to me:

1. How can I have MORE THAN ONE best friend forever, let alone INFINITY best friends forever if—by the very definition of the word *best*—there can be only ONE that is better than the rest, which is what makes that BFF the BEST?

2. Why would I want to have fun with my enemy? If my enemy is so awesome to be around, why are we enemies? Wouldn't we be friends?

3. Am I throwing the PARTY!!!? Or am I merely expected to get invited to and attend the PARTY!!!? Is it deeper than that? Like, do I need to go through junior high with a PARTY!!! attitude like the most popular 8th-Grade Hots, who bounce around the halls shouting "WOOOOOOOOOOOOT!" even when there doesn't seem to be anything worth celebrating?

4. Okay. This one makes sense to me. I love candy. I'd never underestimate the peacemaking properties of candy. Candy is good. The problem is, I've never seen

my sister actually eat anything even vaguely resembling candy, which makes me think that maybe I've got this all wrong.

5. But there *TOTALLY IS* an *I* in *clique*. Even when it's misspelled like "click," which is how I used to write it in elementary school because that's what the word *clique* sounds like. Not "clee-KAY" or "clee-KWAY," which is how you'd think it would be pronounced with that *q-u-e* arrangement and everything. And while on the subject of weird foreign spellings, here's an FYI: *Faux* rhymes with *foe*. I found this out the hard way when I once mispronounced *faux* so it sounded a little too close to another four-letter word, which made my mom threaten to wash my mouth out with soap.

So. Uh. Anyway. Where was I? Oh yeah. My sister had MESSED WITH MY HEAD. Again.

Even worse? I asked for it this time! I can only hope that the path to ultimate me-ness is more straightforward—and less mortifying—with this second IT List than it was with the first!

Chapter Three

I met my best friend at the bus stop the next morning. And before I could eke out a "Hey, Bridget," she was launching herself into full-on emergency mode.

"BURKE IS BREAKING UP WITH ME."

Burke is Bridget's boyfriend. They flirted with each other from the first day of school but made their relationship official, like, only a few days ago. Could it really be over so quickly?

"He hasn't responded to any of my messages. He must be breaking up with me! Why else wouldn't he respond to my messages?"

She flopped backward onto a wooden bench. It was her signature despairing move. I've seen it countless times before, but never over a boyfriend.

"Maybe he accidentally dropped his phone in the toilet," I suggested. "Remember when that happened to me last year and I didn't pick it up when you called because EW! GROSS! PEE! and you thought I was mad at you for seeing *Girl Power 5* without me?"

"But you *were* mad at me about that!"

Whoops! She was right. Bad example. I scrambled for another theory.

"Burke has a dog, right?"

Bridget nodded.

"Remember in fourth grade when my grandmother gave us walkie-talkies and Bowzer buried yours in the backyard and you couldn't find it? And when you didn't respond to my calls I panicked and thought you'd gone missing and Gladdie called the police...?"

Bridget's eyes went wide with panic.

"You think Burke's gone missing? Should I call the police?"

"No!"

"Then why are you telling me to call the police?"

"I'm not! I'm just..."

I'm just really, really bad at dealing with breakup freak-outs.

But as bad as I am, I was grateful Bridget was having this conversation with me at all. I'd known Bridget forever, but she and Dori Sipowitz had gotten superclose since they both made the CHEER TEAM!!! Dori had taken over as Bridget's preferred go-to friend in times of crisis. Currently, I'm her buck-up backup plan. But maybe with some effort I could slip back into the number one spot.

So I tried another tactic.

"What happened the last time you talked to him?" I asked. "Don't spare any details."

Little did I know just how many details wouldn't be spared. Because Bridget gave me ALL THE DETAILS, even the ones that didn't seem relevant, like what flavor gum she was chewing when she waited for Burke at his locker because, apparently, according to Bridget's logic, the difference between strawberry and spearmint can make or break a relationship, which is TOTALLY BONKERS. Even so, I went along with it, if only because that's what seems to be required of a friend in these situations.

"Maybe you should consider cinnamon next time," I found myself suggesting.

"Cinnamon! That's genius! But maybe too spicy? And what about—YAY! The bus!"

The arrival of the bus is always very exciting for Bridget for one very important reason: Burke is on it. And despite—or maybe because of—the breakup freak-out, today was no different. Bridget could barely wait for the vehicle to come to a complete stop before hopping on board. Our bus driver has the impressive ability to yell in full sentences with her teeth clenched on a toothpick; Bridget gives her the opportunity to exercise this skill on a regular basis.

"HEY NOW, BLONDIE! I ain't run over a kid yet, and I don't wanna start with you."

As usual, Bridget ignored Miz Carbone, raced down the aisle, and sprang like a kitty cat into the seat beside Burke.

"I missed you!" Bridget said.

"Yeah," Burke replied. "Me too."

And just like that: The breakup freak-out was over.

Fortunately, Bridget and Burke sit together in the very back of the bus. I sit in the middle of the bus, which is just fine with me because I'd toss my pancakes if I accidentally caught Bridget and Burke... you know.

Kissing.

Ack.

That's one reason why I don't see myself having a boyfriend anytime soon. I can't handle it when Bridget even hints around at what it's like to... you know.

Kiss.

Ack.

I know I'm immature.

So I don't mind sitting by myself on the bus ride to

school. I prefer it, actually. It's really the only time of day I have totally to myself, which is kind of funny because I'm surrounded by chaos. Nobody takes notice of me, and it's pretty easy to get lost in the noise. I stare out the window and get into a zone and think about things, sort of like what my mom says it's like to meditate. Except my mom wears these silky pajama-like things, and I wear fleece. She inhales citrus-scented candles, and I breathe in fart and armpit. She listens to Gregorian chants, and I have a seventh-grade freestyler who calls himself the next Jay Z.

But other than all that, it's totally the same.

For the rest of the short ride to school, I thought about how I'd known Bridget longer than I've known anybody outside my family. But she's so much harder to really know anymore, since she literally turned pretty overnight.

It's important to mention that I'm not misusing *literally* the way *some* of my friends do when they say things like, "I'm *literally* dying of boredom from this conversation" or "I'm *literally* going to explode out of my jeans because I ate that potato chip." Those would be the correct uses of *literally* only if Manda snored herself to death and Sara went *BAM!* like a denim bomb. *Literally* means the exact opposite of what most people—and my friends in particular— think it means. I once made the mistake of trying to correct Manda and Sara by explaining that what they really meant was *figuratively*. It didn't go well. The only flaws Manda and Sara enjoy discussing are the imaginary ones they obsess over in the mirror—and only when they're the ones pointing them out.

"You're the world's biggest word nerd," Manda had chided.

"Omigod," Sara had agreed. "Literally."

"Yeah," Manda had concurred. "Like, literally."

In that instance, I couldn't dispute their use of *literally*. I can't prove it, but it is quite possible that I am indeed the world's biggest word nerd. It annoys my friends, but at least I make my Language Arts teacher happy when my Nerd Self edges out my Trying to Be Normal Self.

Anyway. So I was thinking about Bridget and how she'd always lived across the street. Maybe we wouldn't be best friends—or friends at all—if she lived anywhere else. This wasn't so far-fetched when I considered what happened with Dori Sipowitz the summer before fifth grade. Up to that point, she'd been the third member of our inseparable elementary-school crew, 3ZNUF. Then she moved across town, and Bridget and I pretty much forgot all about her... that is, until she and Bridget reunited as the newest members of the Pineville Junior High CHEER TEAM!!!

My mom's in real estate, and she is always going on about how successful buying and selling is all about location, location, location. I was starting to think location was equally significant in friendships. Location, after all, was the only reason Bridget talked to me about Burke at the bus stop. If she lived across the street from Dori, no doubt that she'd be having her breakup freak-outs with her.

I can't exactly blame her for choosing Dori over me for boyfriend advice. Dori has one major qualification that I do not: an actual boyfriend. Shortly after Bridget and Burke had made it official, Dori had coupled up with Scotty Glazer, one of Burke's football team friends who's only a seventh grader but considered worthy enough to have certain privileges usually reserved for eighth-grade jocks and the girls—like Bridget—who are "lucky" enough to be their girlfriends. What privileges? Back-of-the-bus-sitting privileges and cafeteria-line-cutting privileges and get-out-of-my-way-when-I-walk-down-the-hall privileges. The sort of privileges of popularity that don't seem like a big deal until you see those privileges being enjoyed by NOT YOU.

Dori and Scotty are kind of a surprising couple. Scotty's well-known for his athletic and academic accomplishments; Dori's only sort of known as the plainest girl on the CHEER TEAM!!! who is best friends with the prettiest girl on the CHEER TEAM!!! I swear I'd never seen Scotty speak to Dori before they started going out. And to be honest, I'm still not sure they had a conversation even *after* they started going out. Whenever the four of them are together—which is pretty much all the time—it seems like all the talk is between Bridget and Dori, Burke and Scotty. From what I can tell, "going out" means holding hands when you walk to and from class together but not actually talking to each other or otherwise acknowledging the existence of the person on the other end of your hand. And also, I suppose, you know.

Kissing.

Ack.

I know. Seriously immature. For the record, I don't have a problem with kissing in general. It's just when I think about, like, *specific* kissing, involving *specific* people I've known since elementary school, that I get all immature and ACKED out.

I need to work on this.

So we pulled up in front of the school, and I saw Dori and Scotty waiting on the sidewalk in front of our bus's assigned spot in the parking lot. Sure enough, they were holding hands but not talking. Dori was bouncing on her toes like the arrival of our bus was an early Christmas, Hanukkah, and Kwanzaa all combined into one awesome holiday for all. Then again, she could have been bouncing to keep herself warm. Like Bridget, she refuses to wear a jacket over her red, white, and blue CHEER TEAM!!! uniform, and it was unseasonably chilly for the second week in October.

As a middle-of-the-bus rider, I exit before Bridget and Burke. This is a daily source of annoyance for Dori, who is always DYING to catch up with Bridget. Dori's family has a strict no-technology-after-7:30-p.m. rule in their household, and she just can't wait to dish on all the many, many major events that have occurred since then.

"Hey, Jess," Scotty said as I passed the couple.

"Hey, Scotty," I said.

Scotty's the only seventh-grade football player who scored high enough on the entrance exam to get into the Gifted & Talented classes. More important, he's already almost as tall as Burke. When so many of us girls are growing much faster than the boys, tall goes a loooong way for a guy. Anyway, I don't spend my time thinking about Scotty, but he's fine. And by *fine*, I mean, "Scotty's an okay guy, I guess" and not, like, "Dag, Scotty is so *foyyyyyyyyyne.*"

THIS IS AN IMPORTANT DISTINCTION FOR REASONS THAT WILL BECOME CLEAR SOON ENOUGH.

"Did you finish the science lab?" Scotty asked.

"Yeah," I said.

"Cool," he said.

Three truths about this conversation:

1. That was it. The entire conversation.
2. It was longer than any conversation I'd ever heard between Scotty and his own girlfriend.
3. I repeat: THAT WAS IT. THE ENTIRE CONVERSATION. And I mean that LITERALLY.

At the time I didn't think Dori and I were on bad terms, but we weren't on the best terms, either. I wasn't sure what terms we were on, really, or what we had in common other than a shared history with Bridget. So now you might begin to understand why I thought my sister's IT List could come in handy even if the only part that made sense to me was *candy*.

There didn't seem to be any good reason for me not to greet Dori when she was standing right in front of me. Ignoring someone standing right in front of you requires way more effort than making the polite, normal-person choice of saying "hey." So I said, "Hey."

"Hey, Dori."

Nothing.

Dori doesn't mind making the effort to ignore me. Since she and Bridget have become friends again, she seems determined to prove that 2ZNUF for her. For some reason, this only made me more determined than ever to get a reaction out of her. So I jumped up and down and waved my arms.

"HEEEEEEEEY, DORI."

Scotty laughed.

"Oh, um, hey." Dori didn't take her eyes off the bus. "What's—YAY! YOU!"

And then Dori went back to ignoring me and ran over to hug Bridget, but she didn't drop Scotty's hand and he got pulled along like a puppy on a leash. Judging by the helpless look on Scotty's face, I couldn't help but think that's how he felt around his girlfriend in general: always a few steps behind. I could relate. It was only my second month of junior high, and yet I felt like I'd already fallen so far behind my best friend that I'd never catch up.

Life moves so much faster in seventh grade than it had in sixth. But nothing—NOTHING—sprints around the halls of Pineville Junior High as swiftly as a rumor. As I'd find out for myself less than five minutes after that conversation with Scotty, it's pretty much impossible to get and stay ahead of gossip.

Chapter Four

Sara D'Abruzzi begins every day with an announcement.

"Omigod!"

She always uses the same attention-getting *HUSH! HUSH!* tone whether her news is important ("Omigod! We're having a pop quiz in Spanish today!") or not important in the least ("Omigod! My earlobes are fat!").

However, Sara's latest announcement caught me off guard because it came in the form of a question. One I'd been asking myself lately.

"Omigod! We're friends, right?"

"Uh, yeah," I said. "We're friends. Of course we're friends."

We're friends because her last name is D'Abruzzi and my last name is Darling. It's our alphabetical destiny for her to sit in front of me in every single class (except Wood-shop, THE CLASS I'M NOT SUPPOSED TO BE IN). Her locker is also right next to mine, so we don't even get a break from each other before and after classes.

"As your friend," Sara said, leaning in and lowering her gaze, "I want you to know that I'm, like, totally on your side."

Sara is funny and always says what's on her mind. She also has the lowdown on everyone and everything and loves sharing all the deets with her more (ahem!) clueless friends. But the nonstop gossip makes me uncomfortable. I like her more when she isn't being catty. For an all-too-brief moment I thought Sara was making an effort to be the version of herself I prefer.

"Me too," I said. "I'm on your side."

Awww. Sara and I were having a moment.

ONLY WE TOTALLY WEREN'T.

"OMIGOD! Why? Who's on the other side? Is it Manda? Is she mad because I bought the jean jacket she wanted? WHAT DO YOU KNOW AND HOW DO YOU KNOW IT BEFORE I DO?"

I tried to calm her down.

"I don't know anything about anyone or any sides," I said. "I swear!"

She looked at me skeptically, so I appealed to her superior information-gathering skills.

"No one gets the truth faster than you do, Sara."

As Pineville Junior High's undisputed princess of gossip, this made perfect sense to her.

"You're right," she said, finally relaxing. "Which is why you are so lucky to have me on your side."

Again, she was putting herself on my side. Which meant that there had to be someone else on the other side. I didn't know who that person was, and I didn't want to find out. Unfortunately, Sara was delighted to share that information with me whether I wanted it or not.

"I mean, if you ask me," Sara began, despite the fact I hadn't asked her because I DIDN'T WANT THE ANSWER, "you're waaaay better than Dori...."

"Dori? This is about Dori? What did I do to Dori?"

Then Sara—SARA! Of all people!—shushed me.

"You don't want *everyone* to know," she said, loud enough for *everyone* to hear. "Do you?"

"KNOW WHAT?"

It came out louder than I'd intended. Now *everyone* really was looking at us and listening to us. I lowered my voice to a whisper.

"I have no idea what you're talking about...."

And then our cranky homeroom teacher, Mr. Armbruster, came skulking into the room all stealthlike because he wanted to catch us misbehaving. His favorite thing in life is to punish seventh graders before eight a.m. Sara immediately shut up and spun back around in her chair before she could clear up my confusion. I poked her in the shoulder to try to persuade her to turn around and finish what she'd been about to say, but she just shook her head like, "NO WAY," because Mr. Armbruster had already given her detention twice (for not shutting up and for not facing forward in her chair), and Sara didn't dare to spend any more time in detention with Mr. Armbruster because he is THE WORST.

So the rest of homeroom was torture.

"Good morning, Pineville Junior High!" said the voice of our school principal, Mr. Masters, speaking through the school's PA system.

I was too busy staring at the back of Sara's head to pay much attention to the morning announcements.

"And it's a *grrrreat* morning for the girls' cross-country team...."

I was studying Sara's dark curls with such intensity that I almost convinced myself I'd be able to see past all the hair and look right into her brain if only I focused just a little... bit...harder....

"Jessica Darling!" Mr. Armbruster croaked. "Stand up!"

Everyone in the class was looking at me again. Except Sara. I'm pretty sure she thought it was a trap set by Mr. Armbruster just as an excuse to give her detention again.

"STAND UP."

I was reluctant to stand up. However, I was even more reluctant to find out what sort of punishment Mr. Armbruster would dole out if I didn't. So I stood up.

Then my homeroom teacher did something totally unexpected.

He smiled. And started clapping.

"Congratulations to you and the rest of the girls' cross-country team on your victory!"

Yesterday our team had ended our forever-long losing streak. I was proud of myself and my teammates, but I'd been too busy trying to read Sara's mind to enjoy the public celebration of my first-ever athletic triumph.

"Oh," I said. "Uh. Thanks."

"I was a long-distance runner myself in my youth...."

Seriously, the only thing worse than having a cranky old teacher like Mr. Armbruster dislike you is having a cranky old teacher like Mr. Armbruster like you too much. Every minute he went on and on about his cross-country glories was another minute Sara knew something about me I didn't know myself. When the bell finally rang a BAZIL-LION MINUTES LATER, I couldn't get out of there fast enough. And I mean that in the most literal way because Mr. Armbruster blocked the doorway as I tried to slip past him. Unfortunately, he wasn't finished reminiscing just yet.

"And that's how I beat the legendary Kicky McGhee...."

I could only watch helplessly as Sara darted down the hall, surely telling everyone in seventh grade whatever it was she hadn't gotten around to telling me.

Chapter Five

We were starting a Shakespeare unit in Language Arts, but the theatrics had already begun outside Miss Orden's classroom.

"Omigod, Jess!" Sara gushed. "DRAAAAAMAAAAA."

"Don't worry, sweetie," Manda said as she gently patted my arm. "Sara told me everything about your situation."

That was exactly what I was worried about.

"How could Sara tell you everything about a situation that doesn't exist?"

"Denial!" Manda and Sara said simultaneously.

Then they high-fived and chanted "Bee-Eff-Effs!" which is what they do whenever they say the same thing at the same time.

This happens a lot.

That is, when they're actually speaking to each other.

Manda and Sara are interested in the same things: boys, being popular, and bossing people around. But they often get into fights and make up and LOVE and HATE and LOVE and HATE and LOVE each other many times throughout a single day, which can be very exhausting to keep up with. On that morning, however, they were definitely BFFs. So far.

Manda took off her glasses and polished the lenses with the hem of her pink V-neck. She put them back on again and gave me a pensive look.

"Come on, Jess. You can trust us. We're on your side."

Sara nodded vigorously. "I was just saying how you're so much better than Dori," she said. "Like, it's not even close."

Aha! If Dori was on one side and I was on the other, there could only be one person in the middle: Bridget! This was about Bridget! No wonder Manda and Sara were getting themselves involved. They do not like Bridget. At all. When she made the CHEER TEAM!!! and they did not, Manda and Sara took it very personally, as if it were somehow Bridget's fault that they showed up five minutes late and got kicked out by the coach before tryouts even began.

"It's not a competition," I began.

"Puh-leeze, sweetie," Manda said, twirling her shiny dark blond hair.

"Omigod! Everything is always a competition."

For Manda and Sara, this is totally true. After all, they had founded the Spirit Squad solely for the purpose of proving that their rivals on the CHEER TEAM!!! did not have a monopoly on peppiness or—more important— popularity. Despite the tension between all of us, I still held out hope that we could put our differences aside. And to prove it, I decided to encourage Manda and Sara with my positive example.

"Bridget can be best friends with whoever she wants to be friends with," I said. "She doesn't have to choose between me and Dori."

IT List #1: 1 BFF < 2 BFFs < 4 BFFs < 8 BFFs < INFIN-ITY BFFs

Sara and Manda exchanged looks. Then they burst out laughing.

"This isn't about you, Dori, and Bridget, sweetie," Manda said in her most patronizing voice. "I mean, who cares about Dori and Bridget?"

"Not me!" Sara said, shooting her hand in the air a little too eagerly to prove her point. "I don't care!"

"Well, if this isn't about me and Bridget and Dori, then who—"

And then, because she couldn't keep it to herself for another second, Sara shouted, "OMIGOD! IT'S ABOUT YOU AND SCOTTY!"

And then I reacted in the only logical way.

"Har dee har har."

"We saw you," Manda said.

"*I* saw them," Sara said defensively. "You wouldn't even know if I hadn't told you."

"Saw us *what*?" I asked.

"Omigod! Flirting when you got off the bus this morning!"

"I wouldn't have believed it if I hadn't seen it," Manda said.

"Um. Excuuuuuse me," Sara said, eyes narrowing. "But you *didn't* see it. I saw it."

Sara wasn't kidding when she said *everything* was *always* a competition.

Manda plastered a sweet smile on her face.

"I've seen things, too, you know," she said. "I just don't feel the need to blab all about it."

Oh no! This was not the time for a BFF breakdown. Not when I needed them to provide me with vital information.

"Listen, you two! This is important," I said, stepping between them. "I wasn't flirting! We were just talking! About the science lab!"

Manda and Sara exchanged "yeah, right" looks.

"It's a total scandal," Sara said, rubbing her hands together with glee. "The Scotty Scandal."

"W-w-what?" I sputtered.

"Are you a genius at playing dumb?" Manda asked. "Or are you really this clueless?"

And before I could even contemplate that very legitimate question, Scotty himself elbowed his way through our group and into the room.

"I'm pretty sure this is a fire-code violation," Scotty said to us as he passed.

Sara waited until he was three steps away before going into a full shout.

"OMIGOD! DID YOU SEE THAT?" Sara asked. "DID YOU HEAR THAT?"

I honestly had no idea what she was getting all shouty about.

"Did I hear and see what?"

"He elbowed you first," Manda explained. "And he called you hot."

"He didn't call me that!"

"Yes, he did," Manda said knowingly.

"Duh! The fire-code joke," Sara said.

I still wasn't following.

"Fire is hot," Manda and Sara said.

Same time. "Bee-Eff-Effs!" High five.

"That doesn't mean he was calling me hot," I protested.

Manda and Sara shook their heads sadly because I was

so hopeless. Then the bell rang, and our waifish Language Arts teacher, Miss Orden, clapped her delicate hands to get our attention.

"Greetings, hallway lingerers!" she sang out. "It's time to learn the language of Shakespeare!"

And as we took our seats, Manda snorted in my direction. "It's time *you* learned the language of *boys*."

Manda had it all wrong. I needed to learn the language of *girls* because nothing they were saying made any sense to me. And my most reliable Manda/Sara translator/interpreter hadn't shown up for class.

"Where's Hope?" I said, mostly to myself.

Sara was—as usual—sitting directly in front of me, so she took it upon herself to answer.

"Omigod, she's totally sick," she said. Then, quieter: "I think."

"I think" is the disclaimer Sara tacks onto the end of a sentence when she doesn't really know something, but she wants us to think she does. I hoped in this case Sara was wrong—that Hope wasn't sick and she'd show up any second.

Without really thinking, I turned around to glance at Hope's empty seat. YIKES! I made eye contact with Scotty, who sat two seats behind me. YIKES! I flinched. YIKES! I forcefully flung myself into an oh-so-obvious about-face. YIKES!

Scotty's typical boy obliviousness was the only thing saving me from utter humiliation. He had no idea we were at the center of a seventh-grade scandal that had already been named after him. He had no reason to suspect that my weird behavior had anything to do with him. He could just assume that I was acting weird because that's how I am. Weird.

Boys. So clueless. And so lucky.

"Flirt it up, flirty," Manda joked from two rows over.

I wanted to scream: *I'M NOT FLIRTING. I DON'T EVEN KNOW HOW TO FLIRT. AND THERE'S NO ONE I WANT TO FLIRT WITH EVEN IF I DID.*

I wish Hope had been there. She's known Manda and Sara forever, and she always knows just the right thing to say to shut them up. The most impressive thing about Hope? She never needs to raise her voice to be heard.

Miss Orden took her spot at the front of the class. "Who's ready for *Much Ado About Nothing*?" she asked.

Ha! I was more than ready for the Shakespeare comedy. I was already living it.

Chapter Six

My day went from bad to THE WORST in Español.

I was trying so hard to avoid eye contact with Scotty that I tripped over Sara's huge handbag that she always puts in the aisle like she wants someone to trip over it just so she can say something like, "Omigod! Watch your step! Do you have any idea how much this cost?"

Which is exactly what she said.

"Omigod! Watch your step! Do you have any idea how much this cost?"

"Trip it up, trippy," Manda joked.

And then Señora Epstein said, *"En Español, por favor."*

This is what she always says, and it's RIDICULOUS because we've only been taking her class for a month and we've barely gotten used to introducing ourselves with our Spanish names. (Mine is *Yessica*, with a *Y*.)

So I didn't blame Sara and Manda for just holding up their hands like, "Nope." But I did blame Sara for putting her bag in the aisle. And I also blamed Manda for using my blunder as an excuse to spread her new catchphrase, "Verb it up, verby." They're supposed to be my friends. They should've taken it easy on me, knowing I was already stressed out about The Scotty Scandal.

Anyway. So Señora Epstein turned to me and said, *"¿Estás bien, Yessica?"*

What happened next is totally my fault. I should have kept it simple by saying *"Estoy bien"* meaning "I'm fine." But my Nerd Self insisted on outdoing my Trying to Be Normal Self. I just had to show off my superior Spanish language skills and maybe prove to everyone that The Scotty Scandal wasn't affecting me one bit. So I said, *"Estoy embarazada."*

Señora Epstein looked like she was going to throw up. Then she did the most shocking thing ever. She spoke in English.

"You're WHAT?"

"I'm embarrassed," I said, getting more embarrassed by the millisecond.

"Whew!" She sighed in relief. "You're *embarrassed!*"

"That's what I said. *Embarazada.*"

In an instant, Señora Epstein's grimace turned into a grin, then back into a grimace again, because she was trying hard not to laugh at me. Very, very hard. So hard that her face went from green to red, *verde* to *rojo*.

Then she turned to the class and spoke slowly and deliberately.

"*Ella se siente avergonzada. No es embarazada.*"

The whole class was lost. She returned her attention to me and translated.

"*Embarazada* means…"

(AND I'M DYING AT THE MEMORY OF IT BECAUSE I GET ACKED OUT ABOUT JUST KISSING AND I ACCIDENTALLY TOLD EVERYONE I WAS…)

"…pregnant."

(ACK. ACK. A BAZILLION TIMES ACK AND FOREVER ACK UNTIL INFINITY ACK. ACK. ACK.)

The entire class cracked up, but nobody laughed harder or longer or louder than Manda and Sara. I swear it was almost like the two of them had invented the Spanish language just to set me up for this joke so they had an excuse to make STUPID-GROSS FACES at me and Scotty for the remainder of Spanish and Pre-Algebra and Physical Science and Social Studies and Gym. They didn't see this as acting stupid and gross. They saw this as "just having fun."

"If you can't have fun with your friends," lectured Manda after I asked her for, like, the bazillionth time to stop it already, "who can you have fun with?"

I wanted to point out that they had confused "having fun" with "making fun." And then I remembered IT List #2: Have fun with your enemies. Were Manda and Sara my friends? Or my enemies? On days like this, it was really hard to tell the difference. I must have been contemplating this question pretty deeply because that's when Sara said, "Frown it up, frowny."

Manda was triumphant. With Sara's help, it wouldn't be long before every seventh-grade girl was saying this thing she had just made up that morning.

So at that point I COULDN'T TAKE IT ANYMORE. I had to get away because it was seventh period and Dori would also be in the cafeteria for lunch and I knew Manda and Sara would go out of their way to rev up the rumors about me and Scotty by acting stupider and grosser and "verb it up, verbier" than ever. I skipped out on the cafeteria and ate lunch in the nurse's office.

"This place is full of germs," Nurse Fleet cautioned. "Eating here isn't sanitary. It's not good for your health."

Fortunately Nurse Fleet is also Coach Fleet, head of the girls' cross-country team. Every day at practice she brings out the fierce, determined, and talented athlete in me, a side that no one—not my parents, my sister, my friends— has ever seen before. Myself included. And I guess that's what made me feel like I could be honest with her in a way I couldn't be with any of my teachers.

"So, Coach," I said, "what if I told you eating in the cafeteria today wasn't good for my *mental* health?"

Coach Fleet agreed to let me stay and eat lunch at her desk, which was apparently less germy than the rest of the infirmary. I was kind of hoping she'd ask me what was going on in my life because I kind of felt like telling her. But she didn't ask, because she had to give a talk to a class of eighth graders about the importance of personal hygiene practices called "Deodorant: USE IT."

By last period, I still had a lot of frustration to get out of my system. Luckily I had a hammer and a reason to use it.

Chapter Seven

BAM!

I hit as hard as I could.

BAM! BAM! BAM!

It felt so good to go off like this.

Manda.

BAM!

Sara.

BAM!

Scotty.

BAM!

Dori.

BAM!

I never thought I'd say this: Thank goodness for Wood-shop. Who knew pounding nails into a board could be an awesome stress buster?

BAM! BAM! B—

My Woodshop teacher caught the hammer in midair.

"Take it easy," Mr. Pudel warned. "What did that poor piece of pine ever do to you?"

Woodshop is the only class I don't have with Manda, Sara, Scotty, Dori, or anyone else I know from school. While all my friends are bonding and baking in Home Ec, I'm risking life and limb in Mr. Pudel's Woodshop. It is my so-called elective, but there isn't anything "elective" about it. Industrial Arts had been forced upon me by the mysterious Masters of Scheduling, and I hated it.

At first.

But on a day like the one I'd had, it was a relief to get away from all the drama. Woodshop is a drama-free zone mostly because I'm the only girl in the class. And as Scotty so clearly illustrated earlier, guys don't get involved in drama—even when they're right at the center of it— because they have no idea it's even going on.

I can be someone different in Woodshop than I am the rest of the day. Not like I'm being fake, exactly. I'm just a different part of myself when I'm surrounded by all the Woodshop boys and not with the G&T crew. I even go by a different name in this class. We *all* go by different names because our teacher, Mr. Pudel, is...well...eccentric. He claims to have a medical condition that makes it impossible for him to remember names, which doesn't make any sense because he has no problem remembering our nicknames: Mouth, Cheddar, Squiggy.

"Yo, Clementine."

I'm Clementine. As in "oh my Darling."

"Yo, Aleck."

He's Aleck. As in Smart Aleck. Or Dumb Aleck. Depending on his mood. I know his real name—Marcus Flutie—and he knows mine. But in Woodshop, we're Clementine and Aleck.

Aleck picked up my battered project and pointed to a crack I had hammered into what was supposed to be the fourth wall.

"This birdhouse should be condemned."

He was right. I was feeling better than I had all day, but my birdhouse was definitely worse for the wear. It certainly wasn't fit for occupancy by any flying feathered creature.

Aleck put down the birdhouse and gave me a serious look.

"It's obvious what's happening here," he said.

Oh, just what I needed. Another person telling me what was happening in my own life.

"You're obviously still suffering from PTSSD."

Nothing Aleck ever says is "obvious." Especially when he claims it is so obviously obvious.

"Post-traumatic seagull stress disorder," he explained. "Bird rage."

Aleck is the only student besides Bridget who knows of my secret history as the school mascot, Mighty the Seagull. There's nothing in life he seems to enjoy more than reminding me of that fact. He put his hand comfortingly on my shoulder, as if I were in deep distress.

"It's okay, Clem," he said. "You're safe. You're not trapped in the bird head anymore. The goose can't get you now. Take deep breaths...."

I shook his hand off my shoulder and picked up another hammer.

"Har dee har har."

I reversed the tool and went about removing the fourth wall. If I carefully pried the nails out of the floor, maybe I wouldn't have to start over from scratch.

"So," Aleck said. "You and Scotty Glazer, huh?"

CRRRRRRRRRAAAAAAAAACK!

Aleck took a huge step backward.

"Whoa."

I'd yanked so hard with the hammer claw that the birdhouse broke right in two.

"You heard about me and Scotty? How did you hear about me and Scotty?"

Aleck raked his hands through the mess on the top of his head. It had taken me a while to figure this out, but his hair color comes closest to the reddish-brownish wood stain called Timber Berry. I had used it on the napkinholder project that had come after the spoon and before the birdhouse. I'd gotten a C minus on the spoon and a B minus on the napkin holder, so I held out hope I could earn an A minus on the birdhouse. This would bring me up to the academic standards I was accustomed to.

"Word gets around," he said finally.

"Whatever you've heard isn't true!"

Aleck crossed his arms, covering up the No Fear logo on his T-shirt. "Shouldn't you wait to hear what I've heard before you go around denying it?"

He had a point. I guess.

"What have you heard about me?"

And he opened his mouth and *BOOOOOOOM*! But it came out like a ventriloquist because it wasn't Aleck who was booming but Mr. Pudel.

"ALECK! I NEED A STATUS REPORT ON YOUR BIRDHOUSE."

And then—without so much as acknowledging that we were right in the middle of a VERY IMPORTANT CONVERSATION—Aleck darted over to the drafting table and unrolled an elaborate blueprint, like something an architect would draw up. It would've been impressive if it weren't so totally unnecessary.

"What is this?" Mr. Pudel asked, half-amused and

half-annoyed. He had gotten to know Aleck well enough already to predict that he'd try to outdo the birdhouse assignment without really doing it at all.

"It's the plans I drew up for a housing project," Aleck said proudly. "I call it the *Condor*minium...."

Aleck is the first student in the history of Woodshop— heck, maybe the history of any subject ever—to boast an F plus average.

"I wish you could just complete the assignment as it's given to you," Mr. Pudel said, rubbing his beard wearily. "What have I told you time and again?"

"Just because I can do something doesn't mean I should," Aleck said dutifully.

"So you did hear me," he said. "I thought I wasn't talking loud enough."

Mr. Pudel is even louder than Sara. He's pretty much impossible to ignore, which is important information for understanding the significance of Aleck's dis.

"Just because something's loud enough to hear," Aleck said with quiet confidence, "doesn't mean it's worth listening to."

Yikes. I don't have to tell you how Mr. Pudel responded, because I'm sure you heard him for yourself wherever in the world you were at the time.

"OUT OF MY WORKSHOP. PRINCIPAL. NOW."

I think Mr. Pudel was a bit too harsh on Aleck. He didn't deserve to get detention for insubordination. In my opinion, Aleck's words were the wisest I'd heard anyone say all day.

I was more relieved than ever to hear the final bell ring. I still had cross-country practice, but the worst of the day was finally over. Somehow, despite all the day's many head messings, I'd thought ahead and brought all my homework and running gear with me to Woodshop so I could dodge Sara at our lockers. I really couldn't handle any more speculation on The Scotty Scandal.

I was about halfway to the changing room when two identical voices called out to me, using the nickname they'd heard my dad shouting at our meets.

"Yo, Notso!"

"Hey, Shandi," I said to the twin with the silver beads in her hair.

"Yo, Notso!"

"Hey, Shauna," I said to the twin with the gold beads in her hair.

The Sampson twins aren't just two of the most popular eighth-grade girls; they also happen to be two of the nicest. Other Hots go out of their way to make 7th-Grade Normals like me feel lower than scummy smudges of gum on the cafeteria linoleum. Shandi and Shauna have greeted and treated me like an equal from the moment I showed up at my first cross-country practice. But after the day I'd had, you can't blame me for assuming that they, too, would start messing with me about Scotty.

"So," Shauna said. "How are you feeling today?"

"How do you *think* I'm feeling today?" I snapped back.

"Chill," Shandi said. "We just thought you might be sore after running so fast yesterday."

Yesterday's victory felt like it had happened a bazillion years ago. The Scotty Scandal had completely taken over my life, and yet Shandi and Shauna seemed to know nothing about it. They weren't looking at me any differently. And they certainly weren't making any stupid-gross faces. Maybe this HUGE DEAL that had made me so preoccupied and paranoid all day wasn't important to anyone outside my very small seventh-grade social circle.

"Oh. I'm sorry. I had a crappy day," I replied. "And my shins are killing me."

If Shandi and Shauna were bothered by my bad attitude, they didn't let it show.

"You know how to recover from that?" Shandi asked.

"A long, slow distance run," Shandi answered.

We took a few steps together before I asked for clarification.

"Will running help my shins or my bad day?"

The twins looked at each other before responding. "Both."

And then they took turns giving my ponytail a playful yank before we headed into the changing room to get ready for practice.

That afternoon we ran as a team. Coach Fleet, the Sampson twins, Padma, Molly, and I took an easy jog along the winding trails behind the school's property. They did most of the talking, except for Molly, who is a girl of few words. I listened for a little bit, but mostly I let my mind wander. The others were so engaged in their conversation that they didn't seem to mind that I was there but not *really* there, if that makes any sense. I mean, I was alone with my thoughts, but I didn't feel alone because I was surrounded by my teammates. It was a safe place to be.

So the Sampson twins were right. As a form of therapy, a long, slow distance run was even better than pounding nails. Never before had I been so grateful for the cross-country team. Running is the only part of my life where I'm making any obvious progress.

Chapter Eight

I came home tired. Almost too tired to deal with what happened next.

"Hello, gorgeous!" called a voice from the back of the house.

"Gladdie?!"

I headed straight for my grandmother's favorite place in the world: the kitchen. The whole house already smelled like chocolate and sugar and butter and all things delicious.

"Well, look at you," she said, waving a batter-splattered spatula like a magic wand. "You rapturous thing, you!"

Gladdie had made herself at home. Her silvery perm and sunshine-yellow pantsuit were dusted in a fine coating of flour and cocoa powder. Yes, my grandmother happens to be one of those old-fashioned grannies who loves

to bake and knit, but she has not-so-old-fashioned hob-
bies, too. Truthfully, Gladdie is pretty cool for an eighty-
something-year-old lady with two hip replacements and a
closet full of polyester. She's a champion card player and
performs with a senior citizens' synchronized-swimming
troupe called the Golden Mermaids. She also wears red lipstick at all times. Even in the pool.

"Gimme a hug!"

I complied, figuring it wouldn't matter if I got flour and
cocoa powder and red lipstick all over my already-filthy
running clothes. After a good squeeze, she took a step back
to get a look at me.

"You're more beauteous than ever!"

Gladdie is the only person on the planet who calls me
gorgeous, rapturous, and beauteous even when I am sweaty,
muddy, and smelly after running in the woods for an hour. I'm
fairly sure she believes this only because she's my dad's mom.
With my dark hair, brown eyes, and lanky build, I've always
taken after that side of the family. Of course, it's also possible
that she believes in my beauteousness because she's half-blind.
Like, legally. It's officially on her driver's license, which I guess
means that as long as you aren't *whole*-blind it's totally okey-
doke to drive all the way from Florida to New Jersey.

"Gladdie, what are you doing here? I thought you
weren't coming until Thanksgiving!"

"What? You're not happy to spend a week with me right now?"

She poked me in the upper arm. Gladdie was sassing me. She gives good sass.

"You know I'm happy to see you. I'm just surprised is all." I paused. "My parents know you're here, right?"

"Of course your parents know I'm here," she said. "They're the ones who asked me to come keep an eye on y—"

She sucked in a mouthful of air like she wanted to take back the words and swallow them down.

"KEEP AN EYE ON ME?" I shouted. "BECAUSE I'M A BABY WHO CAN'T LOOK AFTER HERSELF?"

How insulting. Seriously. I'm not a toddler anymore. I'm practically a teenager, and my parents still treat me like I'm barely out of diapers.

"No one thinks you're a baby," Gladdie said firmly. "On the contrary, your parents are very aware that you are growing up quickly. You're becoming a young lady."

I flinched, as I always do when someone refers to me as a "young lady." It's almost more cringe-worthy than being called a baby.

Gladdie went on. "This is a very important time in your life. And it just so happens that your mother and father are both very busy at work right now. They thought it would be best if there was an adult presence in the house."

"To *babysit* me."

"To *be there* for you," she said with a smile.

Okay. So maybe my parents were acting more concerned than condescending when they dispatched Gladdie to *be there* for me.

"So how long are you going to *be there* for me? A week, you said?"

I guess it came out snottier than I intended because Gladdie shot me a reproachful look.

"Looksie, gorgeous," she said, planting her hands squarely on her artificial hips. "Why stay mad at them when you can get excited about me? And how much I'm going to spoil you over the next two weeks?"

"Two?" I said. "But you said—"

She pulled a Tupperware container off the counter, opened the lid, and swirled it under my nose like I've seen my parents do before they drink wine in a fancy restaurant. The scent of caramelly-peanutty goodness took my breath away.

"Are those...?"

"What, these? These Coca-Cola Cap'n Crunchies?" she asked with mock nonchalance. "Otherwise known as..."

"JESSICA *BARLINGS*?"

Before I knew it, my mouth was crammed with the gooey secret recipe my grandmother had created around my two favorite vices. Running made me ravenous, and my mother wasn't around to stop me from stuffing myself with this cookie/brownie hybrid named in my honor. As I *mmmmmmm*ed in appreciation, Gladdie pulled up a stool and sat down. She patted the stool next to her. She wanted to talk. Gladdie has a knack for striking up conversation when my mouth is full.

"So where's 3ZNUF?" Gladdie asked. "Come out, girls!"

She looked behind my back as if I was somehow hiding Bridget and Dori like a magician keeping a rabbit under his cape. It had obviously been a while since Gladdie's last visit. She still thought we were all BFFs. How could I possibly bring Gladdie up to speed on three years' worth of friendship breakups and makeups when I wasn't even sure how to process it all?

"About Bridget and Dori…" I began.

"I made the Platinum Blondies Bridget loves so much," Gladdie said, still squinting around the room. "And Dori's favorite PB & Jellyrolls."

"3ZNUF isn't really a thing anymore," I tried to explain.

Gladdie dipped a Jessica Barling into a cup of tea.

"I mean, I'm still friends with Bridget, and sort of friends with Dori, but mostly because she's still friends with Bridget, too, because they're on the CHEER TEAM!!! together and…"

I'd barely launched into the whole situation when Gladdie stopped me.

"Whoo-wee. We have a lot to catch up on, don't we? Good thing I'm here for three weeks."

"Three weeks? You said two weeks!"

"Eighteen days," Gladdie said. "Split the difference."

I had to laugh. Whether it's fourteen, eighteen, twenty-one, or a bazillion days, we wouldn't have nearly enough time to deal with all my drama. I sighed and was about to very theatrically rest my head on the countertop, but I couldn't because all the available space was taken up with sweet ingredients.

And just like that, it came to me.

IT List #4: When all else fails...

"Hey, Gladdie," I said with a smile. "Can you help me make some candy?"

Chapter Nine

I went to school the next day with more homemade candy than a Wonka family reunion. Right away I offered some to Bridget at the bus stop.

"Gladdie's in town!" I announced. "We made these chocolates."

They tasted as good as they looked. We'd used Gladdie's cookie cutters. Each tiny chocolate was shaped like a bird and lightly dusted in crystals that caught the light. Bridget eagerly reached inside the open bag, then just as quickly withdrew her hand.

"I totally want one," she said, "but school pictures are later this week."

"So?"

She pointed to a piece.

"Is that sugar?"

"Salt," I clarified.

Bridget wrinkled her nose.

"The saltiness intensifies the sweetness."

I was repeating the line Gladdie had used after I'd expressed doubts about salting perfectly delicious dark chocolate.

"The saltiness intensifies the sweetness," Gladdie had said. "Just one of the ways baking is a lot like life."

One of the advantages of being eighty-something is that people actually take your wisdom seriously. However, Bridget was totally unimpressed by Gladdie's words when they came out of my twelve-year-old mouth.

"Salt makes me puffy," she said. "And chocolate causes pimples."

"I think that's a myth," I said, not actually knowing if it was a myth or not.

"Just how many of these have you eaten?"

And before I could answer, she poked at a sore spot under my mouth.

"Owww!"

I didn't even know I had a zit on my chin, which goes to show you just how much time I devote to gazing at my appearance in the mirror each morning.

As the bus approached, Bridget had a sudden change of heart.

"You know what? I'd love some candy!"

I happily handed over one of the mini bags of chocolate Gladdie and I had carefully tied together with red, white, and blue ribbons. Those are the Pineville Junior High School colors. I thought it was a nice touch that Bridget seemed to appreciate.

"Thank you soooo much!"

I was so busy marveling over my sister's IT List wisdom and envisioning how candy could have a similarly positive effect on Manda and Sara that I missed the obvious: Bridget didn't want the candy for herself.

"Lookee, Burke!" Bridget squealed as she bounded onto the bus. "I've got a prezzie that's almost as sweet as you are!"

Ack.

During the ride to school, I prepared myself for a particular set of parking lot obstacles named Dori and Scotty. I knew the couple would be waiting for Bridget and Burke in their usual spot on the curb, and I didn't want to chance any innocent chitchat that could be misinterpreted by Sara or Manda or anyone else without anything better to do than MESS WITH MY HEAD.

Anyway, I was eager to put The Scotty Scandal behind me. So I planned to rush right by Dori and Scotty with just a quick little wave, as if I had crucial homeroom business to attend to. Not unfriendly, but not flirty, either. Just, you know, normal and no biggie.

BUT WHEN IS MY LIFE EVER NORMAL AND NO BIGGIE?

I stepped off the bus and put one foot in front of the other, you know, walking the same way I've been walking since I was ten months old. Only this morning, advanced walking was apparently beyond my skill level because I got TOTALLY TRIPPED UP ON A TEENY PATCH OF GRAVEL ON THE SIDEWALK.

It was one of those slo-mo moments.

I could feel (*Ohhh nooo I'm falling!*) and see (*Ohhh nooo I'm falling on the sidewalk in front of the entire school!*) and fully experience (*Ohhh nooo I'm falling on the sidewalk in front of the entire school and—WHOOSH!—Scotty is catching me and I'm not falling anymore!*) what was happening.

But I was powerless to stop (*Ohhhhhh noooooo!*) it.

"Gotcha!" Scotty said, pulling me back to my feet.

Over his shoulder, Sara was already giving me a thumbs-up. She obviously thought I had orchestrated the whole trip and fall just so I could end up in Scotty's arms. And from the sour look on Dori's face, I could tell she thought it, too.

"Uhthanksbye!" I grunted before dashing away.

Sigh. So much for my effort to put The Scotty Scandal to rest.

Sara was bouncing up and down at our lockers, just

dying to review the event in detail, millisecond by excruciating millisecond.

"Omigod! You fall for Scotty and he falls for you!" Sara gushed.

I wanted to protest, but she wouldn't let me.

"Manda's totally right," Sara went on. "You're an expert flirt!"

Me? An expert flirt? Ha!

Then again, Manda and Sara would know better than I do.

"Seriously," Sara said. "You need to give me some tips!"

Was it possible that flirting was like running cross-country? Maybe it was an untapped talent someone else needed to point out to me. Had Bridget picked up on my powers when she was once (WRONGLY) convinced I had the hots for Burke? NO. NO. NO. The whole idea of me being a secret boyfriend-stealing genius was absurd. I couldn't listen to another word of this ridiculousness!

"HERE." I thrust chocolates in Sara's face. "CANDY."

I might not have succeeded in winning Bridget over with sweets, but I wasn't ready to give up on IT List #4 just yet. Sara reeled back as if I were offering her a bag of flaming dog poop.

"Omigod! Are you trying to make me fat?"

"No!" I protested. "My grandmother and I…"

"Like I won't have enough temptation with Halloween coming up?" Sara griped. "Some friend you are!"

Sara stomped away and refused to acknowledge me for the rest of homeroom. It wasn't the strategy I'd intended, but it certainly was an effective way to make Sara shut up about The Scotty Scandal.

Some friend indeed.

I wondered how candy might work on Manda. I bolted from homeroom so I could get to her in Language Arts before Sara did. My speed work at cross-country practice paid off.

"Hey, Manda," I said breathlessly when I caught up with her in the hall. "Want some?"

"You made this?" she said. "I thought you were more of a Woodshop kind of girl."

Manda thinks it's a laugh riot that I'm in Woodshop.

"Well, my grandmother Gladdie helped me," I explained. "My parents are both working late hours, so she's staying with us."

Manda's eyes lit up.

"Wait. Are you saying your grandmother is the only one standing between you and throwing the ultimate sleepover?"

Nothing could be further from the truth. I could think of a bazillion roadblocks between me and throwing the ultimate sleepover, not the least of which being that I'm not much of a PARTY!!! thrower despite the pressure I was feeling from IT List #3's all caps and triple exclamation points. Then again, maybe party throwing was another hidden skill just waiting to be discovered. That intriguing concept and the fact that we weren't talking about The Scotty Scandal made this conversation totally worth continuing.

"Party…" I said noncommittally.

Sara caught up to us and was feeling very left behind in the conversation.

"Party? Whose party? What party? Where? Why? Is it a themed party?"

Manda ignored her and continued.

"I mean, if your grandmother is anything like my grandmother, she'll pass out in front of a cop show right after dinner," Manda said. "And if your parents are stressed with work, they'll barely even notice we're there. We can stay up late and do whatever we want!"

"Omigod! Whatever we want!" Sara echoed.

Heads were turning all around the hallway. People wanted to know about this party and the seventh grader who was going to throw it.

"Gladdie is pretty sharp for a grandmother," I said. "She's no pushover, either. And she has more energy than I do."

"Sure, sure, whatever," Manda said blithely. "So Friday night—"

I broke in before she could go on. "Actually, it has to be Saturday because I have a meet on Friday afternoon and..."

Manda exhaled testily. "Fine. Saturday night. And it's me, you, Sara, Hope—"

"Hey," I interrupted again. "Is Hope back in school today?"

"Nope," Sara answered. "She's got a stomach thing. Omigod! I hope I don't get it from her, because I'm, like, a really bad barfer."

I was going to ask what made someone qualify as a good barfer when Manda cleared her throat loudly.

"Excuuuuuuse me, sweeties," Manda said, smiling tightly. "I wasn't finished with the guest list for our slumber party."

My slumber party had become "our" slumber party, which might have been annoying if it wasn't such a relief. Manda could take over the whole shindig if she wanted to.

"So," Manda said, ticking off each name on her fingers. "It's me, you, Sara, Hope."

"Right," I said. "Got it."

And then she added, all supercasual, "Oh, and Bridget."

Did I hear that correctly?

"Did you say Bridget?"

"Yes! Me, you, Sara, Hope, and Bridget."

"Bridget," I repeated. "Bridget Milhokovich."

"Of course I want Bridget to come!" Manda said. "Why wouldn't I want Bridget to come?"

"Maybe you wouldn't want Bridget to come because you kind of hate her?" I offered.

"Jess! You couldn't be more wrong," Manda insisted.

"Dori's the one we don't like," Sara clarified. "She's not on the guest list, right, Manda?"

"Oh, no way," Manda answered dismissively. "She's such a try-hard."

"A what?" I asked.

"A try-hard," Manda repeated.

A try-hard. It took me a moment before I got it.

Everyone wants to fit in. But there's a fine line between wanting it and wanting it too much. The quest for popularity has to appear effortless. Even if—*especially* if—you worked very, very hard at it because you wanted it very, very much.

Like Manda and Sara.

"So Dori is out," Manda declared. "But Bridget is definitely in. I, like, literally love Bridget to death!"

And as Manda swept into the classroom, I couldn't help but think that she wasn't misusing *literally* this time. If it were up to Manda, she *would* love Bridget to death.

A slow, painful death.

Thankfully, Manda and Sara were so excited about this hypothetical party I was throwing that they seemed to forget all about The Scotty Scandal. I made it through Language Arts and Español without any reason for them to make stupid-gross faces at me. I was even able to forget my EMBARRASSING blunder from the day before.

That is, until Señora Epstein assigned us our homework.

"Memorize this list of fake cognates," she instructed.

She went on to explain that cognates are foreign words that look and sound similar to English words, so they're easy to figure out. For example:

- *causar* = to cause
- *falso* = false
- *problema* = problem

Fake cognates are tricky. They also look and sound like English words but have totally different definitions than what you'd assume. For example:

- *bizarro* = brave
- *exito* = success
- *pretender* = to try

Obviously Señora Epstein assigned this work sheet because of my humiliating *embarazada/avergonzada* mix-up.

"False cognates are also known as false friends," Señora Epstein said as she passed out the work sheets. "You think they're helping you out, but they're not."

The work sheet was titled "¡*Cuidado! Falsos Amigos Causan Problemas.*"

"Watch out," translated Señora Epstein as I hurried past Manda and Sara and Scotty on my way out the door. "False friends cause problems."

Ha! In more ways than one.

If Hope had been there, I probably would've said that out loud. But she was absent again, so I had to settle for making this little in-joke to myself.

"Woo-hoo! Jess!"

Bridget was waving at me from all the way down at the other end of the hall, which was weird because I never see her in this part of the building after second period. Even from far away, I could see that her face was pink with panic. I assumed whatever had brought her there must be important. We hurried to meet each other halfway.

"What's going on?" I asked. "Are you okay?"

"I'm freaking out!" she said. "And only you can help me!"

It had only been a day since Bridget had come to me in emergency mode, but it felt nice to be needed by her again. And okay, if I'm being totally honest, it felt even better that she had chosen me over Dori.

"Of course!" I replied. "What can I do?"

"I need more candy." Pause. "For Burke."

I should've known better. I didn't want or need to know why this was so important. Without resisting, I reached into my backpack and handed over another bag.

"So, Bridget, are you free on Saturday? Because I'm having a sleepover and..."

Bridget was peeking into my backpack. "Saturday? Um...yeah. I think so." Then she gave me a hopeful look. "Can I have, like, *all* the bags?"

She was acting weird. This was weird. Maybe I was paranoid, but it almost sounded as if Bridget's attendance at my slumber party depended on whether I gave her the rest of the candy.

"Burke likes the chocolate that much?"

"Totally!" she said. "He loved it!"

"Okaaaaaaaay."

I sensed Bridget had more to say.

"Well, he loved the candy so much that I sort of told him that I was the one who made it."

Wait. What? Whoa.

Bridget...lied? I couldn't process this. Bridget never lied. About anything. Ever. The closest Bridget has ever come to lying is forgetting. Like, she'll say something didn't happen that totally happened but only because she doesn't remember it happened until I remind her. That makes her a little ditzy, but not a liar. But why would Bridget be

65

dishonest about something so...dumb? But from the desperate expression on her face, it was clear to me that she saw this situation as anything but dumb.

"Pleasepleasepleasepleaseplease," Bridget begged. "And remember! I made them! Not you!"

I nodded and silently handed over the rest of the bags of chocolate.

"Thankyouthankyouthankyou!" Bridget gushed as she crushed me with a hug. "I'll totally be your best friend forever!"

As Bridget took off in search of her boyfriend, it hit me: That was the first time in twelve years of best friendship that I had to do something to earn the title I'd always taken as a given.

Chapter Ten

When I got home from school, Gladdic had a fresh batch of lavender lemon bars waiting, which sound nasty, but I promise are quite delicious once you get over the idea of eating flavors you associate with dish detergent and potpourri.

"So. Uh. Gladdie?" I began. "I was kinda wondering…"

"What is it with your generation?" Gladdie asked.

"Uh…what?"

"All those 'sos' and 'uhs' and 'kindas' are unbecoming of a dynamic young woman such as yourself," she said. "Be direct! Say what you need to say!"

Just say what I need to say. HA! As if it were that easy. Because what I needed to say was: *I'm under pressure to host a sleepover this weekend, and I'm being bossed into inviting certain friends and not others, and according to my sister's latest IT List, I'm supposed to care about parties and cliques and being Hot and not being Not, but all I really care about is everyone getting along with everyone else.*

But what I said instead was this: "I want to have a sleepover this weekend."

"What a marvelous idea!" Gladdie exclaimed. "I'd love to catch up with Bridget and Dori!"

Bridget would come, if only to get her hands on more candy. And Dori was pretty much forbidden by Manda to come, though I couldn't see any reason why she would want to be there anyway, even if she had made the guest list. That is, unless she, too, had been advised by someone to have fun with her enemies.

"Do you think Mom and Dad will mind?" I asked.

"Your parents will be pleased as punch," Gladdie replied. "They want you to develop positive female friendships."

Something about the way she said it indicated that she'd had a long conversation with my parents about my need to "develop positive female friendships."

"It was actually my friend Manda's idea," I said. "And there's another girl, Sara."

"A party!" Gladdie said, rubbing her hands together with gusto. "I love parties!"

"And one more girl," I said. "Hope."

"The more the merrier!"

Isn't that the philosophy behind IT List #1: 1 BFF < 2 BFFs < 4 BFFs < 8 BFFs < INFINITY BFFs? I could take care of that and IT List #3: PARTY!!! at the same time! I've made so much progress since the first day of school, haven't I? I'm doing a much better job at rocking my sister's Must Dos this time around. Looks like Bethany Darling's little sister is finally getting the hang of this junior-high thing!

"Woo-hoo!" I cheered.

"Woo-hoo!" Gladdie cheered back.

I needed to call Hope about the sleepover right away. As I dialed her number, I realized I'd never called Hope before. I'm not much of a phone person, but I was in the mood to actually *talk* to Hope instead of bleep-blooping messages back and forth. I guess she felt the same way because she sounded pretty psyched when she picked up.

"Hey, Jess!" she said. "I'm so glad you called!"

"How are you feeling? Sara said you had a stomach thing...."

"Yeah, sort of," Hope said vaguely. "Anyway, I'd finally gotten my strength back and was feeling so much better when Manda gave me orders for custom-made handcrafted invitations for the Awesomest Sleepover Ever."

Yikes. That's a lot to live up to.

"Did she really call it that?"

"She did. Oh! And I have to finish them by tomorrow morning for distribution before homeroom."

"Are you serious?"

Hope laughed. "Totally serious."

This was taking bossiness to a whole new level, even for Manda.

"Why do we even need invitations?" I asked. "Everyone invited already knows about it."

"Aha! Knowing Manda, the invitations aren't really about the guests. It's about everyone else."

"What do you mean?"

"She wants everyone who *isn't* invited to see who is invited."

Of course. A selective guest list is what makes a gathering exclusive. Exclusivity is what makes a clique the type of clique that other girls want to get into. Exclusive cliques are for Hots. Everyone else is a Not. This is the total opposite of #1 on the IT List. Sigh. Just when I thought I was making progress.

Anyway, back to the conversation with Hope.

"But if she's so eager to have an exclusive party, why doesn't she just throw one herself?" I asked. "Why put it on me?"

"This way Manda can still be the 'nice' one," she said. "Because you're the one being exclusive."

As soon as she said it, I knew it was true. I actually had to admire Manda's manipulative brilliance. She's by far the MVP All-Star in Girlie Head Games.

But that didn't mean I had to let her outplay me.

"Don't listen to Manda. We don't need invitations," I said. "And you've probably got too much work to make up from your absences."

"I do," Hope said. "Speaking of, what's up with this Spanish work sheet on fake cognates?"

Ack.

"Manda and Sara didn't tell you?"

"Tell me what?"

I thought for sure that they would've already told Hope all about my *embarazada* blunder so they could all "laugh it up, laughy" at my expense.

"Well, it all started when I tripped over Sara's bag...."

"It's like she puts her bag in the aisle just so you trip on it and she can yell at you for tripping on it."

"Exactly! Anyway, so Señora Epstein asked if I was okay and..."

I gave her the whole story. And she laughed. A lot. But that was okay because before long, I was laughing right along with her.

"You should have seen her face when she pointed out my mistake," I said. "It turned green then white then red...."

"Like the flag-of-Mexico sweater she loves so much!" Hope added, and we both cracked up some more.

"So what else have I missed?" Hope asked.

When I'd told Hope about announcing my pregnancy to the Spanish class, the experience seemed more humorous than humiliating. Would the same thing happen if I told her about other stressful stuff happening at school?

There was only one way to find out.

"Did you know I'm in the midst of a scandal?" I asked. "The Scotty Scandal?"

Hope responded with a musical "ooooooh."

"Apparently I'm an expert flirt and Scotty has fallen under my spell."

Hope snorted. "Who thinks that?"

"Manda and Sara," I said. "And Dori, too, I guess, because she's been acting superrude to me lately. But it's not true! I don't like Scotty that way. And even if I did, I'd never go after someone else's boyfriend!"

"I know that," Hope said. "But it's kind of a compliment, don't you think? I mean, you don't see anyone accusing *me* of having that kind of power over boys."

I kindasorta understood what Hope was saying and was about to argue that I'd be way more flattered if everyone was gossiping about skills I actually possessed, like running or factoring polynomials. But that's when my bedroom door flew open.

"BURKE IS BREAKING UP WITH ME."

Bridget flopped backward onto my bed in despair.

"Sounds like you need to go," Hope said.

Though she was trying to be cool about it, I could hear a hint of disappointment in Hope's voice. And that made me even less psyched about wasting the evening coaching Bridget through another breakup freak-out.

"Just give me a second," I said into the phone.

"No," Hope insisted. "It's cool. I'll see you tomorrow." And she hung up.

I stood directly over Bridget, who was as red-eyed and sniffly as I'd ever seen her. Bridget and Burke's relationship was brand-new, but it felt like I'd already talked her through a bazillion breakup freak-outs. Usually I was up for the task of being the good friend who cared about analyzing ALL THE DETAILS. Usually. But not tonight.

"So what if Burke is breaking up with you?" I asked. "Who cares?"

Bridget sat up, shocked.

"Who cares?" she shot back. "I care!"

"What I meant was," I backpedaled, "there are plenty of other guys at Pineville Junior High who'd take Burke's place in a heartbeat."

This is totally true. On the last day of summer before seventh grade, Bridget had gotten her braces off, trimmed her white-blond hair, and bought the right clothes for her curves. Suddenly all the boys noticed her, and she noticed the boys noticing her, and all the other girls in my class noticed the boys noticing her, and...well, that's when everything started to get really complicated.

Bridget sniffed. "I don't want anyone taking his place," she said. "I want the boyfriend I already have. I want Burke."

"Personally, I don't see what's so great about Burke."

"He's gorgeous and popular and plays football. He's perfect!"

Burke smells like deli meat, chews like a cow, and considers farting an art form. (Fart form?) But I didn't say that.

"No one is perfect," I said instead.

"Burke is perfect," Bridget insisted.

"Burke is *tall*," I conceded. "It's not the same thing."

His height advantage doesn't make Burke perfect, no matter what Bridget says.

"If he's so perfect," I argued, "why has being with him made you so paranoid?"

A wounded look crossed Bridget's splotchy face. It would've been less offensive to mention Burke's fascination with farting. I'd obviously crossed some sacred boyfriend/girlfriend line because Bridget stood up stiffly, like a stranger and not someone who'd hung out in my bedroom thousands if not bazillions of times before.

"You just don't understand," Bridget said as she walked to the door. "And until you have a boyfriend, you never will."

I watched her go, wishing she had walked out in silence. What she'd said wasn't untrue. No, it stung because she was so right. I had no hope of understanding what was going on inside my friend's head and heart until I got a boyfriend of my own.

The problem is this: Despite my budding reputation as an "expert flirt," I have zero interest in getting a boyfriend. Especially if it means turning into a girlfriend who behaves like Bridget.

Chapter Eleven

True to form, Bridget didn't acknowledge her breakup freak-out the next morning at the bus stop. She also didn't say anything about how I'm obviously losing patience with her breakup freak-outs, which, quite frankly, is a conversation I *need* to have with her even if I don't *want* to have it.

"So your sleepover is, like, perfect timing because Burke has mandatory team bonding and can't hang out on Saturday night, and it totally works out for Dori because Scotty will also be busy at mandatory team bonding and won't be able to hang out with her, so…"

Uh-oh. I was under strict orders from Manda not to invite Dori, which was convenient for me because I was pretty sure Dori hated my guts because she was under the

TOTALLY MISGUIDED IMPRESSION that I had the hots for her boyfriend.

"Dori's coming?"

"Of course!" Bridget replied. "Duh!"

Then she bonked me on the head with the Official Inflatable PJHS CHEER!!! Wand. On game days, she and the rest of the CHEER TEAM!!! go around bonking students on the head with these *adorable* red, white, and blue blow-up weapons. The CHEER TEAM!!! is actually allowed to do this. I'm not kidding. The administration is totally okay with them physically assaulting the rest of us with cheeritude.

"Gladdie said she couldn't wait to see 3ZNUF back together again," Bridget went on. "Did you know that she was baking all our favorite treats? Platinum Blondies and PB & Jellyrolls? Your grandmother is the best, Jess. And—YAY! The bus!"

For the rest of the ride to school, I tried to figure out why Dori would even want to come to my slumber party when she'd been going out of her way to show that she was not a fan of me lately. It got even more confusing when I got off the bus.

"Heeeeeey, Jess!"

I actually looked around to confirm that I was the person Dori was so happy to see.

"So! Saturday night! Yay!"

"Huh?"

This earned me a bonk on the head with Dori's Official Inflatable PJHS CHEER!!! Wand.

"The sleepover! Can't wait! Woo-hoo! A good old girls' night in while the boys are at mandatory team bonding!" She looked sharply at Scotty when she said that. "Woo-hoo! 3ZNUF! What fun!"

We may not be besties anymore, but I don't dislike Dori. I generally disagree with Manda and Sara when they say mean things about her. However, in this case at least, Dori was proving them right by being such a try-hard. She was putting waaaaay too much effort into sounding excited to spend time with me. The weirdest part about her act? It seemed to be more for Scotty's benefit than for mine. But why?

Bridget bounded off the bus.

"Awwwwww!" she gushed at the two of us. "Together again!"

She linked one arm with Dori's and the other arm with mine. This sounds like no big deal, but it was in fact a HUGELY SIGNIFICANT GESTURE because it required her to unlatch herself from Burke's bicep, if only for a few seconds. And in that brief moment of bonding, I felt kind of bad for being so cynical. Maybe Dori had come to her senses about all the rumors and was ready to rebuild our friendship after all.

Or not.

"So, Scotty!" Dori said emphatically. "We'll all be at Jessica's house on Saturday night while you're at mandatory team bonding. So. Don't! Get! Any! Ideas!"

And Scotty just shrugged and said, "I don't have any ideas," which is probably the truest thing anyone has ever said in the history of the universe.

"It better stay that way!" Dori cautioned.

And then she looked at me like I was supposed to say something, but I didn't know what that something was, because this wasn't making any sense to me at all.

I swear it was like I was hearing half of a satellite transmission of an intergalactic conversation. Like, one part of the discussion was happening right in front of me with words I could understand. But the other half was happening in a galaxy far, far away in an alien language that translated "Hello!" into something like "*Vnpykghtioqew!*"

I guess I waited too long to say whatever it was I was supposed to say because Dori decided to say it for me.

"And don't you get any ideas, either, Jess!" And then Dori released a gust of the most forced laughter I've ever heard. "Ha. Ha. Ha. Ha. Ha. Ha."

And that's when I realized that Dori was paranoid. She

still believed in The Scotty Scandal and wanted to hang out on Saturday so she could keep an eye on me! As if I'd sneak out of the slumber party and Scotty would ditch his team-bonding night and he and I would, like, meet up somewhere in secret and...

ACK.

I was still processing all this when Bridget and Dori untangled themselves from me, picked up their CHEER!!! wands, and bonked me on the head. (It might be my over-active imagination, but I swear Dori bonked me harder than was absolutely necessary.) Then they locked arms with their respective boyfriends; waved giggly, giddy good-byes; and flitted away, leaving me behind to wonder WHAT THE HECK JUST HAPPENED.

"What the heck just happened?" asked Hope.

I spun around and saw her standing behind me on the sidewalk. She was back! I'd never been so happy to see her. I would have hugged her, but I'm not much of a hugger and I don't think she is, either.

"I was attacked by a pack of evil, peppy pixies," I replied. "You know. The usual."

"Uh-oh!" Hope said, sounding genuinely alarmed. "Have you seen Manda or Sara yet today?"

"No," I replied. "Why?"

"Well, your day is about to get worse—oh no!" Hope's eyes widened. "Duck!"

"Wh—?"

But it was too late.

Bonk. SQUEAK! Bonk. SQUEAK! Bonk. SQUEAK!

"What the heck!"

Manda and Sara were laughing their heads off. They were wearing Spirit Squad tees and armed with even bigger blow-up weaponry than Bridget and Dori's.

"You've been struck with the Spirit Squad Squeaky Stick!"

And just to make their point, they hit me a few more times.

BONK. BONK. BONK.

SQUEAK! SQUEAK! SQUEAK!

"Quit it!" I snapped.

Manda stopped.

"Sorry, sweetie!" she said, not sounding at all apologetic. "But that's payback for telling Hope not to make the invitations."

"Omigod!" Sara said. "That was so not cool of you."

"Whatever!" Manda said, all chipper-like. "I'm over it now! Come on, Sara! Let's spread spirit to the hotties on the lacrosse team!"

And then they took off, swinging their Spirit Squad Squeaky Sticks above their heads like they were heading into battle.

Hope and I stood on the sidewalk for a few seconds in silence.

"Be afraid," I said. "Be very, very afraid. The CHEER TEAM!!! and the Spirit Squad are armed and dangerous."

"Don't worry," Hope said. "They'll take it out on each other."

See, there's a limited amount of PJHS pride to go around. The girls on the CHEER TEAM!!! (i.e., Bridget and Dori) dis the girls on the Spirit Squad (i.e., Manda and Sara) by saying things like, "Oh, the only reason girls join the Spirit Squad is because they aren't good enough to be one of us." And the girls on the Spirit Squad (i.e., Manda and Sara) dis the girls on the CHEER TEAM!!! (i.e., Bridget and Dori) by saying things like, "Oh, the only reason they're on the CHEER TEAM!!! is because they know they'd never get voted into the Spirit Squad or pass our supersecret initiation process."

Hope was right. Once armed, neither side would waste time putting their weapons to use. Sure enough, we were blocked by a scrum of students at the front entrance. Everyone was scrambling around one another to get a better look at whatever was going on right inside the doorway. It was obviously something major, too, because everyone was all like, "ooh" and "ahh" and "daaaaag" and "oh man" and, you know, the excited noises we make when we're watching the craziest stuff go down.

"What's going on?" I asked.

Then, over the noise of the crowd, I heard:

BONK! SHRIEK! SQUEAK! BONK! SHRIEK! SQUEAK!

Hope and I looked at each other like, "OMIGOD," because even though we didn't know what was happening, we knew for sure who was making it happen.

"Who's winning? Dori and Bridget or Manda and Sara?" I shouted, pointlessly hopping up and down to try to see over the heads of all the curious onlookers in my way. "Tell me!"

Hope is the tallest girl in the whole school—seventh and eighth grade combined. She had a better view of the action than just about everyone else.

"It's, like, the weirdest thing," Hope said. "They're hitting each other with their inflatables"—*BONK! SHRIEK! SQUEAK!*—"but they're all smiley like it's great fun among besties but..."

BONK! SHRIEK! SQUEAK! SHRIEK!

"But it's obvious they're out for blood," I said.

Hope looked down and smiled wryly. "See? At this rate, they'll be disarmed before our first class. You won't have to worry about having to check their weapons at the door tomorrow night."

Hope was right yet again. The weapons were confiscated before homeroom.

"Omigod! It's so unfair!" ranted Sara when she stormed

into Mr. Armbruster's classroom, her Spirit Squad Squeaky Stick noticeably absent from her grip. "So it was totally fine for the CHEER TEAM!!! to hit people with their stupid wands, but as soon as the Spirit Squad gets our own inflatables, it's suddenly a problem? It's discrimination! I should get Daddy's lawyer on this!"

"Why not just let the CHEER TEAM!!! do its thing and the Spirit Squad do your thing?" I asked. "Why did you have to go after Bridget and Dori anyway?"

"Omigod. About that," she said. "It's all your fault."

"*My* fault?"

"Why didn't you tell us that you'd invited Dori to your sleepover?"

"The more the merrier!" I said, channeling Gladdie and the IT List spirit of infinite BFFs.

"Well," Sara said, "she was getting all braggy about being invited, and Manda was like, 'Sorry, sweetie, it's VIP only,' and Dori was like, 'I know; how did *you* find out about it?' and she bonked Manda on the head with her wand and had this huge fake smile on her face, like she was playing around but really meant it, you know?"

Oh boy, did I know.

"And Manda was like, 'Oh, ha ha ha,' but what she was really thinking was 'I'll smack that fake smile right off your face,' so she whacked Dori on the side of the head with the Squeaky Stick, and the next thing I knew…"

BATTLE ROYAL.

"Omigod! They're jealous," Sara continued. "They're jealous because they're both so clueless, and if they weren't on the CHEER TEAM!!!, they'd still be the clueless girls who sit at the square tables in the cafeteria with all the other clueless seventh graders."

"They're just jealous," Manda told me in Language Arts. "They're jealous because we're Hot and they're Not and that's that."

"They're jealous," Dori told me on the way to buy French fries during lunch. "They're jealous because I'm dating Scotty and they're not and I see the way they look at him and they *better not get any ideas....*"

"They're jealous," Bridget told me on the way back from buying French fries during lunch. "They're jealous because they'll never have a friendship like ours."

"I'm jealous," Hope said when I returned to the table. "Those French fries look deeeeeeelicious."

I happily shared my plate with her. This was the easiest—and only—problem I solved all day.

The worst part about the nastiness Manda and Sara and Dori and Bridget were spreading about each other? Well, besides the fact that I was at the center of it? Some of the smack talk—just a teensy little bit—was possibly true. I could see how Dori and Bridget might envy Manda's persuasive personality or Sara's all-knowingness. I understood why Manda and Sara might wish they had boyfriends like Dori and Bridget or a friendship that went all the way back to the crib.

I just wish they didn't have to be so mean about it.

And that I wasn't in the middle.

Mostly, I wish they'd gone to war *after* the Awesomest Sleepover Ever.

I was so happy to head to Woodshop, where I assumed I wouldn't hear anything about the PARTY!!!

I was wrong.

"So what time should I get there tomorrow night?" Aleck asked.

"What are you talking about?" I asked.

"You're having a party, right?" he said.

I almost asked him how he knew about my social life. But I didn't because I could predict his reply: *Word gets around.*

Does it ever.

"It's a sleepover," I corrected. "A by-invite-only sleepover."

"Oh," he said, slightly deflated. "So." Pause. "Am I invited or what?"

I rolled my eyes. "No, you are not invited."

"But we're friends, aren't we?"

Were Aleck and I friends? We talked every day. We joked around. We helped each other with our work. Did that make us friends?

"That's irrelevant," I said. "You're a boy. You're not invited."

Aleck looked wounded. "That's gender discrimination."

"Get Daddy's lawyer," I joked, remembering Sara's rant in homeroom.

"Nah, too complicated," Aleck said, as if I were making a serious suggestion. "It'll be way easier if I just crash the party instead."

"Har dee har har," I said. "You wouldn't dare."

"Uh-oh!" Mouth chimed in over Aleck's shoulder. "You dared him!"

"I didn't," I said. "And he won't."

"You did," Aleck said. "And I will."

I folded my arms across my chest and stood my ground. "You won't."

Aleck grinned from ear to ear.

"You really don't know anything about me, do you?"

I didn't. But maybe that's why I found Aleck so interesting.

Maybe that's why I wanted to know more.

Chapter Twelve

Let's look on the positive side. There weren't any fatalities at the Awesomest Sleepover Ever.

But we came close.

Too close.

Waaaaaaay too close.

I guess I should go back to the beginning.

I planned the perfect party. With help, of course. Gladdie outdid herself on the food front by setting up a buffet representing the whole sweet-salty-savory-spicy junk-food spectrum. Mom bought out the local drugstore's hair, skin, and nail care departments so we'd have enough assorted beauty products to supply a whole season of TV makeovers. Dad even let me stock up on all the trashiest gossip magazines he usually won't let me read because he claims they'll rot my brain. And when my guests and I got bored with stuffing our mouths, makeupping our faces, and rotting our brains, we had Bethany's collection of classic teen comedies all queued up and ready to roll. Best of all? We'd be pretty much left to ourselves because Gladdie persuaded my parents to enjoy a "date night."

"You need your freedom," Gladdie said. "I'll make myself scarce."

I'd thought of everything. I was determined to be the hostess with the mostest. And yet, despite all my careful preparations, I was still nervous about throwing the Awesomest Sleepover Ever. Gladdie sensed it, too. Five minutes before the girls were scheduled to arrive, she offered a bit of advice.

"Stick together as a group and keep the private conversations to a minimum. Divide and you will be conquered."

Then she headed to the guest bedroom with her knitting, promising to be neither seen nor heard unless there was an emergency. I'd barely had time to contemplate Gladdie's advice when the doorbell rang. I was really, really hoping (ha!) Hope would be the first to show up. So I was a little disappointed and a lot surprised to open the door to find that Manda and Sara and Bridget and Dori had all arrived at the same time—though it was obvious that they hadn't all arrived *together*.

Manda and Sara shouldered their floral quilted over-night bags and pushed their way past Bridget and Dori and *their* floral quilted overnight bags to get through the door first.

"Can we talk to you alone?" Manda asked, but it wasn't really a question.

"In private," Sara said, eyeing Bridget and Dori. "No offense!"

Two seconds into the sleepover and I was already being lured into the kind of dangerous private conversation Gladdie had warned me about.

"Uh, now?"

"Now," said Manda and Sara simultaneously.

They didn't high-five or "Bee-Eff-Effs!" which indicated that the topic of this private conversation was very serious indeed.

I shot Bridget and Dori an apologetic look.

"You know your way around! Say hi to Gladdie! She's so excited to see you! We'll be right back! Help yourselves to snacks!"

Ugh. I was being such a try-hard.

Manda and Sara followed me to the guest bathroom, and Sara closed the door behind us.

"Omigod! I can't believe she showed! After everything with you and Scotty."

"There is no 'everything' with me and Scotty," I snapped. "Stop saying that."

"I can't believe you invited her," Manda replied tartly. "I don't remember putting her on the guest list."

"I don't remember this being your house or your party," I shot back.

Whoops. Manda doesn't like when anyone questions her authority. Normally I know better than to mouth off, but I was under too much party pressure to consider the consequences. I honestly didn't know how she'd respond to such back talk, so I can't say that I was surprised or unsurprised when she silently turned toward the sink, flipped on the tap, squirted soap into her hands, and lathered up.

Sara and I just looked at each other like, "What the heck?"

Manda rinsed carefully, reached for a towel, and dried off.

"You're right," she said when she was finally finished. "I'm going to take the high road here. And do you know why?"

I didn't know why. And I don't think Sara did, either.

"Because I can."

Then she walked out the door without another word, as if she had literally *and* figuratively washed her hands of the whole Dori situation.

I wasn't the only one who was confused.

"Omigod! What was that about?" Sara asked.

"I have no idea!" I replied. "I was going to ask you!"

"She can be so weird sometimes," Sara said, rolling her eyes. "Right?"

Sara had practically backed me into the toilet at this point, and she just stood there with her hands on her hips waiting for me to agree with her.

"Uh, right?" I said tentatively. "I guess?"

A huge smile spread across her face, like this was exactly what she had wanted me to say, and I immediately got all paranoid that she would somehow use this agreement against me, so I was quick to add something like, "But we're all weird sometimes, right?" but I know she didn't hear me because she was already heading back down the hall toward the party in progress.

When I returned to the living room, Dori and Bridget were whispering to each other over by the junk-food buffet. Sara had already joined Manda on the opposite side of the room. They were messing around with the music. Apparently my retro soundtrack wasn't what they had in mind.

"Wow!" Manda marveled. "Your taste in music is as *interesting* as your fashion sense."

I had dressed for battle in a U2 *War* T-shirt. I didn't need to check myself out in a mirror to know that Manda wasn't paying me a compliment. *Interesting* was synonymous with *icky*. This was Manda's definition of taking the high road? At that point I was already seriously contemplating taking any road that would lead me away from my own sleepover when I belatedly noticed all the guests were in attendance.

"Hey, Hope!" I called out enthusiastically.

"Hey, Jess," she responded less enthusiastically.

Hope had arrived while we were in the bathroom. That was good. She was curled on the couch with a pillow clutched to her abdomen. That was bad. Had her stomach thing come back?

"I'm glad you made it."

Hope nodded feebly, tried to smile, then stuffed a chocolate-covered pretzel into her mouth.

Manda pushed a button, and a bubbly pop song came bursting out of the speakers. The effect was immediate.

"We love this song!" shouted Bridget and Dori.

"Omigod! Who doesn't?" shouted back Sara.

Uh, me? I was obviously the only person in the room who hadn't heard it before. But I didn't care about being left out, because I was so grateful to Manda for giving everyone a reason to get along. My friends all bopped around like they were possessed by aliens from the planet Shakeyerbootie. Well, all but Hope, who didn't get off the couch but showed her appreciation for the song by dipping her head up and down to the beat. Even Gladdie poked her head into the room long enough to say, "Catchy!" before returning to the guest room with her knitting.

And then, just as quickly as the dance party started, Manda shut it down.

"Awwwwwww! Put it back on!" Sara, Bridget, and Dori whined.

Manda set herself up in the center of the room and clapped to get everyone's attention.

"So! Now that we're all here," Manda said. "You can thank me."

"Thank you," Sara replied without thinking.

"Why are we thanking you?" I asked.

"Only because I've come up with the perfect group Halloween costume for us!"

Us? As in all of us? Wow. Maybe Manda meant what she'd said in the bathroom about taking the high road. Maybe it wasn't so impossible for all six of us to get along!

"You did?" Sara asked in a snippy voice. "When were you going to tell me?"

"Um?" Manda replied. "I'm telling you right now. Duh."

"I thought we were gonna, like, discuss it first."

"Puh-leeze. There's no need for discussion," Manda said pointedly. "Because it's brilliant."

"What is it?" Bridget asked, bouncing up and down. "What is it? WHAT IS IT?"

Have I mentioned how much Bridget loves dressing up for Halloween?

Manda stood quietly in the middle of the room, expertly building up the tension before making her announcement.

"We will be…" She paused once more, at her own peril, I might add, because Bridget looked like she was about to pounce on her. "The Chibi Girls!"

Everyone let out little squeals of joy. Even Hope.

"Who are the Chibi Girls?" I asked.

This was such a totally dumb question that they all ignored me.

"I'm brilliant," Manda bragged. "Right?"

Everyone agreed Manda was brilliant. Except Sara.

"When it was *my* idea to be the Chibi Girls, it was dumb," Sara whined. "But now that it's *your* idea, it's brilliant?"

I tried again. "Who are the Chibi Girls?"

"Who gets to be who?" Dori wanted to know.

"Can I be Bouncy Chibi?" Bridget asked.

I stood on top of the ottoman to get their attention.

"FOR THE LAST TIME," I shouted, "WHO ARE THE CHIBI GIRLS?"

"Omigod! We were just *listening* to the Chibi Girls!"

"We were?"

Manda turned the music back on, and all the girls went back to bopping. Then she abruptly shut it off again.

"The Chibi Girls," Manda explained, "are the of-the-moment Japanese pop group—"

"That you hadn't even heard of until *I* showed you their video last week," Sara interrupted.

"There's Bouncy Chibi..." Dori began.

"I want to be Bouncy!" Bridget reminded us.

"You're Beauty," Sara said. "Duh."

Bridget looked disappointed by this, the obvious truth. I didn't even know the Chibi Girls, and it was clear to me that Bridget should be the one called Beauty because, as Sara explained, duh.

"And there's Baby and Brainy and Bashy," Dori said, wrapping up.

"Bashy?" I asked. "Like, she goes around beating people up?"

I immediately thought of an inflatables battle royal.

"Um," Dori said, unsure of herself. "I think it's because she throws parties?" She looked to Sara for confirmation.

"Bashy is slang for 'cool' in Jamaican," Sara explained.

"But I thought they were Japanese." I was totally confused.

"They're musical and multicultural," Hope chimed in from her spot on the couch in that Hope-y kind of way where I couldn't tell if she was joking or not.

"Ohhhh."

And just when I thought Hope might be making a recovery, she asked me to direct her to the bathroom. I pointed down the hall and to the right.

"Are you going to be okay?" I asked.

Hope shrugged.

"You've seriously never heard of them?" Bridget asked when Hope had left.

"Oh, you know Jessica," Manda said. "She only likes the bands on her vintage T-shirts."

"'Giggle Pop'?!" Bridget said helpfully.

And then Manda turned the music back on and, like a command, she, Sara, Bridget, and Dori started singing a song that sounded like this:

"Giggle giggle giggle POP!
HA-ha-HA-ha-HA-ha-HA!
Giggle giggle giggle POP!
HA-ha-HA-ha-HA-ha-HA!"

Repeat until someone—in this case, me—smashes the singers in the face with a piece of confiscated inflatable weaponry. Bashy indeed.

"You're so right, Manda," Bridget gushed. "It really is the perfect group costume!"

There was only one problem. By my count there were five Chibi Girls and six of us at the sleepover. You didn't have to be Brainy Chibi to know who would be left out.

And yet Dori didn't seem to have a clue.

Ack. It was classic Manda to blurt out the details of her brilliant group costume right in front of her, too, instead of waiting for a more appropriate moment so she wouldn't feel excluded. Like, why couldn't Manda have stuck to the high road just a little bit longer? Why couldn't she have waited until Dori had gone to the bathroom before going on about her perfect group costume? Part of me still felt guilty about cutting Dori on the cafeteria line way back on the first day of school. Maybe I could make it up to her right now. I couldn't stop this girl-on-girl crime from happening at school, but I was not going to allow this blatant nastiness to happen at MY SLEEPOVER.

"Maybe we can come up with some other group costume ideas," I suggested.

"Oh, puh-leeze," Manda said, waving me off. "Hope, you're obviously Bashy because of your red hair."

Hope had just emerged from the bathroom and responded to this news with even less enthusiasm than I had.

"Huh?" Hope said in an offhand way. "What?"

"We're going to be the Chibi Girls, and you're Bashy," Manda said.

"Because of your red hair," Sara reminded her, just in case Hope thought for a second it was because she was cooler than they were.

"Right," Manda concurred. "Try to keep up."

Easier said than done. Who could possibly keep up with all the alliances and factions forming and disbanding?

"I'm just saying that we should keep our options open," I said.

"Okay," Manda said, smirking. "Let's hear another option. I would love to hear Jessica's option, wouldn't you, Sara?"

"Yes," answered Sara predictably. "I would."

"How about you, Bridget?"

"Sure!"

"Hope?"

Hope nodded, but I wasn't convinced she'd even heard what Manda had asked.

Manda wouldn't bother asking Dori.

"Okay! An option!"

I didn't have an option. But I had to fill the inevitable awkward silence of Manda NOT asking Dori for her opinion, so I blurted out the first idea that came to mind.

"We can, um, dress up like various elements from the periodic table."

And because no one said anything to stop me, I kept going.

"It's so simple! We all wear matching black leggings and white T-shirts with symbols for our elements written in black letters across the front. Like, Manda, you can be

Pt for platinum. Sara, O for oxygen." The idea wasn't half-bad, really. "Bridget is gold and Hope is neon."

"What about me?" Dori asked.

"Um...helium?"

MOST AWKWARD OF AWKWARD SILENCES.

Followed by riotous laughter.

"Like, it's not enough that you're already getting all As?" Manda asked.

Technically, that isn't true. I have a C plus average in Woodshop.

"Omigod! Only you would come up with a costume to earn extra credit in Mr. Odd's class," Sara joked.

Mr. Odd was actually Mr. Todd, our science teacher who bore more than a passing resemblance to Franken-stein's monster.

"Seriously," Dori said. "Kiss it up, kissy."

Just hinting at Mr. Odd and kissing sent everyone into a second round of hysterics. This proved that the Chibi Girls bonding wasn't a fluke. It *was* possible for everyone at my sleepover to get along...if it was at my expense.

Manda, Sara, Bridget, and Dori had a grand old time picking an element/costume for me.

"Wouldn't Jessica make a perfect lead?" Manda asked the other girls.

"Omigod! Yes! Ld!"

"The symbol for lead is Pb," I corrected Sara automatically. "Not Ld."

"Nerd it up, nerdy!" said Bridget.

"Aha! That's it!" Dori said gleefully. "Jessica is Nd. Nerdium!"

Manda and Sara gawked at Dori like they were seeing her for the very first time.

"NERDIUM!!!"

They were still far from BFFs, but this unexpected stroke of snarky brilliance earned Dori high fives from Manda and Sara. In fact, there was such a feeling of camaraderie going around the room that they high-fived Bridget, too, just for the heck of it.

To her credit, Hope wasn't joining in, but she wasn't doing anything to stop them, either. She was so hot and cold lately. After our phone conversation, I'd been really looking forward to staying up late with her—later than everyone else—swapping stories. But with the way she was acting, I kind of wished she hadn't shown up at all. I was asking myself how I'd possibly make it through the night when a surprise visitor came gliding into the living room on my grandmother's arm.

"Look who crashed the party!" Gladdie called out.

It was Bethany! Right on time to save me!

Chapter Thirteen

I was so relieved when my sister took the spotlight. If they focused on her, they couldn't make fun of me.

"I heard you got the five-foot-four spot in The Alignment," said Bethany to Bridget.

Bethany was referring to The Famous Pineville Junior High Arrow Pointing Toward Awesomeness Alignment. It's been the CHEER TEAM!!! signature formation since my sister's days as captain. Personally, I don't see what's so amazing about arranging yourselves according to height, but I've been told that's because I'm not a CHEER!!! aficionado and therefore unqualified to appreciate a legendary alignment when I see one.

"Yep!" Bridget squeaked.

"And you must have the other five-foot-four spot," said Bethany to Dori.

"Yep!" squeaked Dori.

Bridget and Dori were seriously starstruck. The Chibi Girls have nothing on my sister. Especially when she started talking CHEER TEAM!!! business.

"I was the five-foot-four spot back in the day...."

"YEP!" squeaked Dori and Bridget.

Bridget's an only child, and Dori's the only girl in her family. Growing up, Bethany was like a big sister to all of us. And by that, I mean she was way too busy being impossibly popular and pretty and perfect to pay any attention to three elementary-school kids.

The more she ignored us, the more glamorous we imagined her life to be. We'd act out scenes from her life with our dolls. Bethany was the closest thing to real-life Barbie we'd ever seen.

"Ooh, Ken!" Bridget would make Barbie-as-Bethany say. "I'd love to go for a ride in your convertible!"

"Ooh, Prince Charming!" Dori would make Barbie-as-Bethany say. "I'd love to go to prom with you!"

Bridget and Dori got annoyed whenever I didn't stick to their fantasy script.

"Ooh, G.I. Joe!" I'd make Barbie-as-Bethany say. "I'd love to fight terrorists and save the world with you!"

Anyway, Bridget and Dori have admired my sister since the 3ZNUF days. But I didn't expect Bethany to make an equally glamorous impression on Manda and Sara.

"Omigod! *That's* your sister?" Sara asked.

I couldn't blame Sara for her disbelief.

Me: oversize *War* T-shirt, jeans, sneakers.

Bethany: formfitting cashmere sweater, miniskirt, knee-high boots.

Me: brown hair slipping out of a lazy ponytail.

Bethany: golden hair flowing in perfect waves.

Me: straight up and down.

Bethany: curves in all the right places.

"She's totally gorgeous," observed Manda. "She looks *nothing* like you."

Gee, thanks for the reminder.

Me: my ordinary face.

Bethany: her extraordinary face.

Only Hope was unmoved by my sister's arrival.

"Bethany, dear," interrupted Gladdie, "your gentleman friend requires your attention."

All heads turned toward Bethany's "gentleman friend." We hadn't even noticed he was there until Gladdie spoke up. He was an unnoticeable kind of guy—with a forgettable face and average build. Even his gray hoodie and jeans blended in with the wall he was standing in front of.

"Um, hi," he said.

Bethany has brought home dozens of boys over the years, but none of them resembled this guy. She usually goes for jocks. And jerks. Guys with big muscles and even bigger attitudes. This "gentleman friend" was shy and looked like he hit the books, not the gym.

"This is our neighbor Rodney," Bethany said to the group.

"Rodger," said Rodger-not-Rodney.

"Oh, right," Bethany said.

Aha! Rodger-not-Rodney looked familiar, and not just because he had one of those blendy-in faces. He'd lived in our neighborhood forever! In fact, when my sister was my age, he was the preteen genius she'd paid to build a toddler trap to keep me out of her room! I hadn't seen him in years. He must have been away at college. I remember my parents marveling about his acceptance to one of the big-time Ivy League schools.

"Gladdie, can you show Rodger to the office? He's got some work to do for me in there. I'll join you in a moment."

Rodger-not-Rodney was smart, but it seemed he was still a sucker when it came to my sister. As Gladdie escorted him from the room, I tried to figure out what Bethany was up to. She turned to Manda and Sara.

"So! Are you two on the CHEER TEAM!!!?"

The weird thing about this question is that Bethany already knew the answer was no. I'd told her the whole story about how they'd been dismissed from tryouts by

Miss Garcia because they were too focused on applying many layers of cheer flair to show up on time.

Flustered by Bethany's sudden attention, Manda and Sara got all tongue-tied.

"Not. Like. On. But. Tryouts. So."

"Omigod! The team. Five minutes. And flair."

"Not. Fair."

"Totally. Not fair. At all."

Translation: It was totally not fair that they were dismissed from tryouts because they had been too focused on applying many layers of cheer flair to show up on time.

Manda and Sara were still trying to explain themselves when Bethany coolly turned her back to them.

"Jessie, can you help me with something?"

I wondered why she'd need my help when she already had Rodger-not-Rodney working for her.

"I'll be right back," I assured my guests. "Enjoy the buffet! Browse the magazines! Peruse our movie collection!"

Ugh. Try-hard.

Instead of following Rodger-not-Rodney and Gladdie into the Techno Dojo (aka my dad's office), Bethany led me to her bedroom. She'd barely shut the door behind her before she turned on me.

"What the heck is happening here?" Bethany asked.

"I was going to ask you the same thing about Rodger," I said.

My sister looked at me blankly.

"You mean Rodney?"

"*Rodger*. Not Rodney."

My sister waved my correction away, as if knowing his real name was a nuisance, like mosquitoes at a barbecue.

"He's making minor adjustments to Mom and Dad's computer," she said as she fluffed her hair in the mirror. "To improve the flow of information."

"Why do you care about Mom and Dad's flow of infor—?"

I hadn't even finished asking the question when I came to the answer.

"Aha! He's hacking their accounts to block e-mails from college about how you failed out!"

My sister puckered her lips in the mirror, neither confirming nor denying the charge.

"I don't understand why you just don't tell them the truth," I continued. "They have to find out eventually...."

"Hey, sis, don't change the subject," said Bethany to change the subject. "What is going on here tonight?"

"A party," I replied. "Just like you told me to."

"I can see that," she replied. "And I can also see that you don't like most of the girls you invited."

"Is it that obvious?"

"To someone with my expert eye, of course it's obvious," she said. "So why are these girls here? Especially the new ones who didn't make CHEER TEAM!!!?"

"This is me having fun with my enemies!" I said. "Just like your IT List told me to."

"Ohhh," my sister said, snapping her manicured fingers. "Perfect!"

See? PROGRESS IS BEING MADE.

Or so I thought.

"So what are you going to do?" she said all sneaky-like. "Wait until they fall asleep and give them face tattoos with a Sharpie?"

"No!"

"Or when you're doing makeovers, you could dye their hair a really hideous orange."

"Why would I do that?" I asked. "That will just make things worse than they already are!"

"Well, of course," Bethany said. "That's the downside to having fun with your enemies. They get mad when you mess with them. So you have to be prepared for them to retaliate. Omigod, like, once I talked this annoying girl Julia into plucking off her eyebrows...."

Julia. Where had I heard that name before?

"And then Julia tried to get revenge by inviting me to a sleepover where she had planned all these pranks...."

Wait. What? Whoa.

"Julia?" I broke in. "The same slumber-party invitation with the IT List written on the back?"

"Right! Only I obviously didn't fall for her trick, because no one was better at getting back than I was."

And all at once it dawned on me: My sister wasn't encouraging me to have fun with my enemies. She wanted me to have fun MESSING WITH my enemies.

"You're really good at these power plays. Keep it up; you'll be the queen of the IT clique before you know it."

She beamed at me proudly and strutted out the door to join my grandmother and Rodger-not-Rodney in the Techno Dojo.

My sister was totally wrong, of course. I wasn't good at this stuff at all. And for once, I was grateful to be so socially inept. If I had to power-play my way to having infinity BFFs, I decided right then and there that I was better off alone.

Little did I know how quickly I'd get my wish.

Chapter Fourteen

When I returned to the living room, more than half the party had vanished.

"Where did everyone go?"

"Hope organized a group trip to the bathroom," Bridget replied.

"We weren't invited," Dori added.

Now I was really annoyed. Hope had barely spoken to me all night. Yet the moment I leave the room, she finds the energy to have a private gossip sesh with Manda and Sara? Of all the low blows I'd suffered at my own sleepover, this was the lowest.

So far.

I was wondering how the sleepover could get any worse when I heard the doorbell ring, followed by a riot of giggly squeals.

"EEK!" Manda came running out of the bathroom with Sara close behind. "THE BOYS HAVE ARRIVED! I REPEAT. THE BOYS HAVE ARRIVED."

"What boys?" Bridget asked.

"Puh-leeze." Manda winked at Bridget. "You know what boys."

I don't know why I hadn't figured it out sooner. Boys were the only reason why Manda had insisted on Bridget's presence at my party. If Bridget came, boys would, too. And they did.

"We have more unexpected company," Gladdie announced, ushering the next wave of surprise guests into the living room.

And they really did come as a surprise because they weren't at all the boys Manda and Sara had in mind.

"Hey, ladies," said the wrong boys.

"Ew." Manda curled her lip. "I can't believe it's you."

I couldn't believe it, either. It was Aleck. From Woodshop.

Whoops. I mean, Marcus Flutie, even though I never call him Marcus and he never calls me Jessica. Mouth and Cheddar were standing alongside him.

"Hey, Clem!" they said in unison.

"Who's Clem?" asked Sara.

"Clem's me," I said. "It's kind of a Woodshop thing."

I regretted it as soon as I said it.

"It's a Woodshop thing!" Manda and Sara singsonged mockingly. *"Ooooooh."*

Gladdie gracefully stepped between the boys and the girls.

"You gentlemen are welcome to stay," Gladdie said, "but that requires full participation in all slumber-party activities."

Her blue eyes twinkled with mischief as she left the room once again. If I didn't know any better, I would've thought my grandmother actually *wanted* the boys to stay. Mouth and Cheddar shifted from high-top to high-top, looking like they were ready to bolt right back out the door they had come in. Aleck, on the other hand, stepped forward and took command of the situation. I still couldn't believe he had crashed my party. He'd said he would crash my party, AND HE DID.

"Ladies," he began. "Can you give us a full itinerary of activities so we can make an educated decision as to whether we should stay or go?"

"Puh-leeze," Manda said. "Just go home."

"Omigod," Sara added. "Seriously."

Manda turned to Bridget and Dori.

"I thought you said Burke and Scotty would bring friends for me and Sara!"

Just when I thought that maybe, just maybe, Dori had

put The Scotty Scandal nonsense behind her, she proved otherwise.

"Did you actually think I'd encourage my boyfriend to come *here*?" she asked. "So I could watch Jessica flirt with him? Ha!" Then she quickly looked at me and said, "No offense!"

Ever notice how the rudest insults are often followed by the phrase "no offense!" as if that magical phrase cancels out the dis? I was really regretting Dori's presence at the party. (But not as much as I would later on.)

Manda and Sara were throwing a fit.

"Seriously, Bridget," Manda huffed. "You promised."

"Omigod! You totally did."

"Whoopsie! The boys have a mandatory team-bonding night," Bridget said. "Didn't I tell you?"

I honestly wasn't sure whether Bridget had genuinely forgotten to tell Manda and Sara or had forgotten on purpose. In other words: lie. Manda's and Sara's eyes turned to slits. Their opinion on the matter was clear.

I didn't know whether to laugh or cry. Having boys crash my sleepover would've been very cool, but only if the *right* boys had crashed. Aleck, Mouth, and Cheddar were definitely the wrong boys.

"So what's up first?" Aleck asked.

"There's a dance-off!" Dori offered.

Manda and Sara glared.

Without hesitation, Aleck launched into a pop, lock, and robot.

"Dance-off," Aleck said. "Check."

"And makeovers!" Bridget put out there.

Aleck patted the electric-socket red frizz atop his head.

"I *need* a makeover," he said. "Check."

"And Truth or Dare," Dori added.

"I live for Truth or Dare," Aleck replied. "Truth or Dare is my life. Isn't it, Clem?"

Well, he'd certainly told the truth when he dared to crash my sleepover. And that fact made me dumbstruck with awe and anger and...something else.

"I'll start off with a dare right now," said Mouth eagerly. "I dare you ladies to sneak out with us!"

"Puh-leeze," Manda said dismissively.

"As if," Sara added.

"We know where the Octofire is tonight," Mouth said.

Manda and Sara laughed in the boys' faces.

"You do not," Sara said. "If I don't know where the Octofire is tonight, there's no way you do."

"My brother is the lighter of the torch," Cheddar said.

This got Manda's and Sara's attention.

"The lighter of the torch?" Manda said.

"Omigod! That's, like, a huge honor," Sara said with

genuine awe. "My brother's a senior, and he's never been the lighter of the torch."

"What are you talking about?" I asked.

"Octofire!" answered everyone in the room.

Yes, everyone. Even Hope, who was back on the couch and had barely muttered a word all night long. I'm quite sure that if Gladdie, Bethany, and Rodger-not-Rodney had been in the room, they would have yelled it, too.

"What's Octofire?"

Sara had opened her mouth to tell all when Manda cut her off.

"Having to explain everything all the time is just so…" Manda exhaled deeply. "Exhausting."

Sara nodded, even though explaining everything all the time is pretty much her favorite thing to do.

"The Octofire is always held on the first Saturday after the full moon in October," Aleck clarified. "It's the secret bonfire to celebrate fall."

"If it's such a secret, why do you all know about it, but I don't?"

Everybody looked around the room at one another and shrugged.

"Word of advice, Jess," said Manda smugly. "Spend less time running around in circles with the cross-country team and more time paying attention to the important stuff."

How am I supposed to pay attention to "the important stuff" when I don't even know what it is? And more to the point: WHY DOES EVERYBODY KNOW "THE IMPORTANT STUFF" BUT ME?

Mouth was getting impatient. "Are you in or are you out?"

Manda and Sara looked at each other and came to a mutual conclusion.

"We're in!"

"You're in?" I asked. "Really?"

"Yes, really," Manda said. "We're leaving with the boys."

"Those boys? Mouth and Cheddar?" I gulped. "And Aleck? You don't even know them."

"His brother is the lighter of the torch," Sara said, nodding toward Cheddar. "How bad could they possibly be?"

On cue, Aleck, Mouth, and Cheddar smiled like innocent choirboys.

"Your sister is totally gorgeous, and look at the nerd she was hanging out with tonight," Sara said.

"She's using him!" I cried. "To hack into my dad's computer!"

"Well, no duh! Of course she is!" Then Manda leaned in close so the boys couldn't hear. "Tons of cute boys will be at the Octofire. High school boys. We don't have to stick with—ugh—them."

And then Manda put on one of her biggest, fakest smiles and waved at the boys she was so eager to dismiss. They smiled back because they were, as usual, clueless.

"What am I supposed to tell Gladdie when she asks where you are?" I said. "You're her responsibility, and if something happens to you…"

Manda and Sara rolled their eyes.

"You're, like, literally the old-fartiest girl I know," Manda said.

"Omigod, yes!" Sara agreed. "Gran it up, granny."

And at that point I was so annoyed with both of them, I couldn't wait for them to get out of my house. And quite frankly, I didn't care what happened to them after they did. I led them to the back door so they'd go undetected by Gladdie.

"Just go," I said. "Now."

"Keep the door unlocked," Manda reminded me. "So we can sneak back in later on."

So that's how, just an hour after my slumber party had begun, Manda and Sara were heading out the door with two boys from my Woodshop class who they didn't even know.

That's right. Two.

Aleck stayed put.

"I'm ready for the dance-off," he said to me, Bridget, Dori, and Hope. "And my nails are a mess."

Bridget inspected the chewed-up fingers on his right hand.

"Ew," she said. "They are."

"You're going to miss out on the Octofire—whatever that even is—to stick around here and get a manicure?" I asked.

"Tonight, Clem," he said, "I'm putting the man back in manicure."

Bridget and Dori exchanged confused, curious looks.

"Why do you keep calling her Clem?" Dori asked.

"It's a long story," Aleck and I said in unison.

It sure was. And it was getting more and more complicated by the minute.

Chapter Fifteen

Gladdie came charging into the room holding a tray stacked with fresh snacks.

"More guests require more foo—" She swiveled her head. "What happened to your friends? And don't tell me they're in the bathroom, because it is most definitely not coed!"

The rest of us kind of just looked at one another and held up our half-manicured hands like, "I dunno."

"Somebody better start talking!" Gladdie said with take-no-prisoners toughness.

"They left," I answered truthfully.

"Together?" Gladdie asked. "The girls and the boys?"

"We tried to stop them," I answered less than truthfully, because—let's face it—I'd practically shooed them out the door.

Gladdie wasn't about to waste any time.

"NOT ON MY WATCH," she bellowed, thrusting her fist into the air. "I've still got a friend or two down at the police department. You kids don't worry about a thing. Just go back to enjoying yourselves."

Then she marched away like she was BOSS OF THE WORLD.

"Is she really calling the cops?" Aleck asked.

"Yes," Bridget, Dori, and I replied simultaneously.

We looked at one another and laughed. I knew we were all thinking about the time in second grade when Gladdie called her friends down at the police department when she thought 3ZNUF had been kidnapped ON HER WATCH. We were picked up by the authorities about a half mile away from Wawa. We had taken a vote and unanimously decided that we were totally old enough to buy cherry slushies without adult permission or supervision. We were, evidently, mistaken.

Well, so were Manda and Sara if they thought they could fool my grandmother. It served them right if they got picked up by the police! And I know this sounds totally goody-goody, but I was grateful for my grandmother's interference. Gladdie had taken control of the situation, and the rest of us could just get back to the business of having fun. And for a few moments there, it felt like this could turn out to be a totally normal slumber party. Well, except for one totally abnormal male guest. We'd finish filing and painting our nails. We'd listen to music. We'd munch on Gladdie's delicious junk food....

"What was in those bars your grandmother made me?" Dori rasped.

"I dunno," I said. "Peanut butter and some kind of jelly."

"It. Wasn't. Graaaaape."

Bridget picked a PB & Jellyroll off the tray, broke it in half, and took a tiny bite.

"Strawberry!" Bridget screeched.

"Never. Strawberry. Only. Grape," Dori wheezed.

"I think Gladdie wanted to give you something a little different," I lied.

It had been my idea to mess with the recipe, not Gladdie's. In a weird way, I thought it could be kind of a peace offering. Like, *Hey! You've changed! You're not as boring as grape jelly anymore! You're strawberry jelly!* Not that I actually said any of this to her, of course.

"She's allergic to strawberries!" Bridget yelped. "How could you not know that after all these years?"

She was right. How could I not know that?

"She needs help!" Bridget was on the verge of hysterics. "Help! HELP! HELLLLLLLLLLLLLP!"

"What the h—?" Bethany asked as she ran into the room. "Gladdie's on the phone with the police? And—"

"Dori is dyyyyyyyyyyyiiiiiiiiing!"

This was bad. Really bad. Just minutes earlier, I had contemplated taking a Sharpie to Dori's face in revenge from her "no offense!" offensiveness. Was it possible that I'd subconsciously attempted to MURDER HER WITH STRAWBERRY JELLY?

Thankfully, Dori was tougher than she looked. "I'm." *Wheeze.* "Not." *Wheeze.* "Dying." *Wheeze.*

Dori rummaged through her overnight bag. Very calmly, she removed and uncapped an EpiPen and stabbed herself in the upper thigh—right through her jeans—as if it were the most natural thing in the world. The rush of medicine to her system had an almost immediate effect on her.

"See?" she said, taking a deep breath. "I'm not dying."

But Bridget was inconsolable at this point. She threw her arms around Dori and wept and wailed and went totally bonkers.

"You're my bestie!" she sobbed. "What would I do without yoooooouuuuuuu?"

Well, it was official. I'd been replaced. I don't care what Bethany's IT List says about having infinity BFFs. I had no doubt who Bridget had chosen as her bestest of the best. Dori was number one. And that made me feel like a steaming pile of number two.

"This happened to a girl in my sorority once," Bethany said. "We really need to get Dori home to her parents. I'll drive."

"I'll go with you!" Bridget croaked through her tears. "It's my fault she's here. She didn't even want to cooooommmmmmmme." She barely glanced in my direction before adding, "No offense."

Of course not.

Bridget and Dori grabbed their overnight bags and took off to wait for Bethany in the driveway. The party was officially kaput. It shouldn't have come as a surprise when Hope quietly asked if my sister would drive her home, too.

"I need to be in my own bed tonight."

Hope had been suffering in silence all evening. In fact, I'd kind of forgotten she was even here. But after everything that had happened, I was too angry and annoyed to take anyone's feelings into consideration but my own.

"Oh, go ahead and have fun with Manda and Sara at the Octobofire."

"Octofire," Hope corrected. "And you're joking, right?"

I just glared at her. And when Hope realized I wasn't kidding, she reeled back with shock. It was the most expression she'd shown all evening.

"What? Are you crazy? Noooo," she protested.

"Whatever," I snapped. "Just go."

As soon as I said it, I felt sort of bad for saying it. But

she had already turned away from me and picked up her bag, and it seemed too late to apologize. Besides, I was also sort of peeved at her for being such a bummer. I was, like, half-sorry and half–not sorry. It was a very confusing way to feel.

So Bethany and Rodger-not-Rodney drove Dori, Bridget, and Hope home. That left only one guest remaining. But not for long.

"Get out!" I yelled at Aleck.

"Oh, come on, Clem," he said. "I didn't even get to finish my manicure...."

"OUT!"

Aleck had nothing to do with the sleepover's failure, but it made me feel better to blame him, anyway.

For about a minute.

And then I felt more awful than ever.

Chapter Sixteen

The next morning, Gladdie shook me awake shortly before noon. I should've known she'd never let me sleep the day away.

"Come on," she said, clapping her hands. "Time to clean up your mess!"

And she wasn't referring to the sad, stale, and soggy remnants of the junk-food buffet. I knew she was right, but that didn't make me any happier about all the remorseful phone calls I had to make. To ease myself into it, I decided to start with least sorry and work my way up to most sorry from there.

So I called Manda first to apologize for Gladdie getting police involved. As it turned out, Manda was beyond excited about her run-in with the law.

"Everyone is buzzing about us!"

Wait. What? Whoa.

"So you're really not mad that my grandmother had you picked up by the cops?"

"Mad? It's practically the best thing that's ever happened. I mean, it's not every Saturday night that two seventh-grade girls get taken home in a squad car! We're..." Manda paused before settling on the right word. "*Notorious.*"

And then she said she had to go because *someone* was waiting for her. And that's exactly how she said it, too.

"Gotta go! *Someone* is waiting for me."

Manda put mysterious emphasis on "someone" so I'd be left wondering who this someone was. And even though I know she said it that way on purpose to pique my curiosity, she totally succeeded in piquing my curiosity, which was both annoying and a powerful testimony to Manda's mind-gaming expertise. Ugh.

Next up was Sara. She responded similarly to my call.

"Omigod! We've got, like, *reputations* now. We're *rebels!*"

Sara went on and on and onnnnnnn with each and every detail of their notorious reputation-making rebellion.

"Omigod! It was all so dramatic with the siren and flashing lights of the squad car and all! And the boys took off like, *BANG! ZOOM!* They were outta there! And Manda started bawling like a baby, but I was like, 'Chillax, chick, it's not like we're getting arrested.' The cops just reminded us that there's, you know, a curfew for unaccompanied minors after dark and blahblahblah and then they drove us home."

Funny how Manda failed to mention the whole bawling-like-a-baby part of the evening.

"So your parents aren't mad at you for coming home in a cop car?"

If I ever came home in a cop car, my parents would ground me for infinity.

"Um, actually, they're mad at you and the lack of adult supervision at your slumber party," Sara said matter-of-factly. "Expect a strongly worded letter from Daddy's lawyer."

And then she laughed like this was the funniest thing ever, and I was too afraid to find out if she was joking.

Next up? Dori. I wasn't exactly sure what to say.

Sorry I almost killed you last night.

"Hello?" answered a male voice that was sort of familiar.

"Uh, hello?" I said, uncertain that I'd dialed the correct number. "This is Jessica Darling. I'm looking for Dori?"

"Oh, hey, Jess! It's Scotty."

OF COURSE IT'S SCOTTY. Just add him to my list of apologies.

Sorry I almost killed your girlfriend last night. Oh, and while I have your attention: I DO NOT HAVE THE HOTS FOR YOU.

"Uh. I was kind of hoping I could check in with Dori to make sure she's okay."

"That's really cool of you," Scotty said. "She's still worn out from the whole thing, but I'll ask."

There was a brief muffled conversation followed by the passing of the phone.

"Hello?" Dori asked in a tiny, tired voice that was so much worse than I had expected.

"Dori! Holy cow. Are you okay?"

"Scotty," Dori said in a wheezy voice. "Could you be the best boyfriend ever and get me a glass of orange juice?"

I heard Scotty say, "Sure thing!" followed by fading footsteps.

"Thanks," she said in a hoarse whisper.

"Dori! You sound terrible! I feel terrible!"

Dori giggled.

"Don't feel terrible! This is awesome! I've got Scotty waiting on me hand and foot!"

"Huh?"

"He feels guilty for not being there when I almost died!"

"W-w-what?"

"Don't freak! I didn't almost die! I'm totally fine!" Dori insisted in a low but robust tone. "But Scotty doesn't know that, and you can't tell him, okay? I am loving all this attention! This is the best thing ever to happen to our relationship and—oh! Here he comes with my OJ!"

Dori coughed. "Thanks, hon," she said weakly. "Bye, Jess."

Well. If I'd known accidental near death was all it would take to make things hunky-Dori, I would have smuggled a strawberry into her lunch LONG AGO.

Since Dori wasn't mad about what happened last night, I figured there was no reason for Bridget to hold a grudge, right? Two minutes later, I was crossing the street. I found Bridget wheeling her bike out of the garage. She was wearing workout clothes and a smile.

"Hey! I'm on my way out!" she said. "I'm so glad you caught me!"

"You are?" I asked. "Because I wanted to make sure that everything was okay, you know, after everything that happened at the party...."

"Everything's perfect! Gladdie insisted that I take all the leftovers!"

She unzipped her backpack. It was full of junk food from the party.

"Burke is going to LOVE ME. Thank you! Thank you! Thank you!"

Then she pedaled away.

Wow. These confrontations had gone so much better than I expected. But I wasn't done yet. I had the toughest apology ahead of me. It was the most difficult because I wasn't exactly sure what I was sorry about.

"Hey, Hope," I said into the phone. "I'm—"

"Sorry!" she blurted before I could apologize first. "I was such a bummer last night."

It's true. Hope was a bummer last night. And yet her apology was still unexpected. And, well, unnecessary. It was my PARTY!!! after all. And I felt responsible for everything that happened. I'd been under a lot of PARTY!!! pressure, and I was probably putting out a weird vibe that made Hope feel uncomfortable. It was the first time she'd ever been invited to my house, and I hadn't even been there to greet her when she arrived because I was dealing with Manda-and-Sara drama in the bathroom. That's not cool. So I couldn't blame Hope for creating a little bathroom drama of her own later on in the party. Or, for that matter, bailing on the party altogether.

At least that's how I'd sorted it all out in my head. But she didn't give me enough time to take my share of the blame for her bummer.

"I'm also sorry that I can't really talk right now, okay?" she said. "Bye!"

Then she hung up as quickly as she had apologized.

Huh.

So.

I'd accomplished what I'd set out to do: No one hated me. In fact, four out of five guests seemed to like me even more now than they did before the PARTY!!! And yet, even hours later, I still felt like there was business left unsettled. Maybe it was because my exchange with Hope had mattered the most—and satisfied me the least. Or perhaps it was because there was still one more person I needed to apologize to.

But I didn't know Aleck's phone number. And after the way I yelled at him last night, I doubted he would pick up even if I did.

Chapter Seventeen

After the great success of yesterday's apology tour, I assumed I'd put all PARTY!!! talk behind me. I was wrong. In fact, as far as Pineville Junior High was concerned, the conversation about Saturday night was just getting started.

"You're the girl who threw the party, right?" asked an eighth grader at my bus stop named Jazmin. She wears head-to-toe black, and her eyes are all raccoony from too much eyeliner. It's like she's in the Halloween spirit all year-round and not just in October. So she's kind of scary, is what I'm saying. And she'd never spoken to me before, so her interest took me by surprise. Bridget answered all too eagerly when I didn't reply fast enough.

"She is!"

Jazmin's smudgy eyes bugged out.

"I heard a girl was poisoned! And cops arrested two prime suspects!"

Jazmin was waaay too excited about murder and incarceration.

"I was there!" Bridget chimed in. "It was like, whoa. Intense."

I elbowed Bridget. Why was she encouraging this craziness?

"You know that's not what happened! No one was poisoned. And no one was arrested."

"That's not what I heard," Jazmin said.

"Dori had an allergic reaction to strawberry jelly," I stated. "And Manda and Sara got picked up for being out after curfew. That's it. The whole story."

"I get it." Jazmin winked like we were coconspirators. "You have to say that. To protect yourself."

Then she bowed her head and slowly backed away as a show of respect.

The rest of the day only got weirder from there.

It was impossible to zone out during the bus ride to school because everyone was buzzing about the PARTY!!!

"Dori was unconscious for five minutes!"

"Manda and Sara got handcuffed!"

It was ridiculous. Even Burke got into it, which was a

bit bizarre because up to that point I was pretty sure Burke didn't even know who I was.

"You throw a killer party," Burke said. "Get it? Killer? Heh, heh."

I could tell that he was feeling pretty proud of himself for coming up with this pun on his own. His chest was all puffed out like I was supposed to be awestruck by the fact that he was acknowledging my existence. And I was fine with playing along for Bridget's sake. That is, until he popped a Coco Loco mini into his mouth. A Coco Loco mini my grandmother had invented and I had made with my very own hands for the sleepover. Not that he knew that.

"Mmmmm," Burke said, returning his attention to his girlfriend. "Home Ec is the best thing that ever happened to you!"

And Bridget got all swoony, and I got annoyed. I was so close to telling Burke the truth, but then Bridget gave me a pathetic, pleading look that took all the pleasure out of it for me. Was her relationship with Burke so rocky that she needed to take all the credit for my and (mostly) Gladdie's hard work in the kitchen? IT List #4: When all else fails: CANDY. Maybe this Must Do also applied to boyfriends.

I got off the bus and saw right away that a small crowd had formed around the other IT couple of Pineville Junior

High. Dori was telling everyone about her Near-Death Experience. Scotty stood behind her as if he were ready to catch her if she fell backward into a faint, which was a poor strategy because science has proven that fainters fall forward, but whatever.

"I saw a bright white light," Dori was saying to the enraptured audience. "I was drawn toward it. But then, all of a sudden, something pulled me away, and I came back."

She paused dramatically.

"I guess it wasn't my time to go."

All this drama over strawberry jelly.

STRAWBERRY JELLY.

Dori was too busy being fawned over by a circle of oohing and ahhing admirers to notice me. But Scotty saw me. And I saw him. And in that split second of connection, he unmistakably rolled his eyes at me as if to say "I KNOW MY GIRLFRIEND IS TOTALLY BOGUS." And as much as I appreciated that I wasn't the only one aware of Dori's fakery, there was no way I was about to encourage any more bonding between me and Scotty, because things were messy enough already.

I ditched that scene as swiftly as possible and headed straight for my locker. Halfway there, Hope tapped me on the shoulder.

"Hey."

"Hey," I said cautiously, not knowing what kind of mood she was in. She was smiling, so that was a positive sign.

"Is it me? Or is the entire school talking about Saturday night?"

"I know, right?" I replied. "It's crazy."

And it was about to get even crazier.

Manda and Sara were blocking my locker, holding court to a mixed crowd of seventh- and eighth-grade girls and guys. I was sort of surprised to see Mouth and Cheddar among them. Aleck was elsewhere, which was fine with me because I wasn't ready to apologize to him yet.

"It was like an episode of *COPS!*" Mouth was boasting.

"We saw those flashing lights, and we were like, 'we out!'" Cheddar added.

"Mouth and Cheddar ditched us! We were so mad," Manda said, not sounding very mad at all.

"Omigod! So mad," Sara said, also not sounding very mad.

I was wondering when "Mouth" and "Cheddar" had become their official names outside Mr. Pudel's workshop when the warning bell rang and the crowd dispersed and MANDA AND MOUTH TOTALLY KISSED EACH OTHER.

LIKE, ON THE LIPS.

"Bye, babe," Manda said to Mouth.

"See ya later, babe," Mouth said to Manda.

"MANDA AND MOUTH ARE BABE AND BABE?" Usually all-capsy questions like this stay in my head where they belong. But this one escaped.

"Omigod! You don't know?" Sara asked. "Manda and Mouth are a thing now. And it's all because of your PARTY!!!"

Honestly, the whens, wheres, and hows of this union were unimportant. But I had to know the whys. I approached the new couple, who were still attached to each other despite having already said their good-byes.

"So…you two, huh?" I said, having a hard time looking at them.

"I love the bad boys!" Manda gushed.

"I love her HUGE…" Mouth gestured right at her chest. "Heart."

Manda giggled, and I turned away before they started another round of good-byes.

"Don't blame yourself," Hope said, sympathetically patting me on the shoulder.

She knew I didn't want credit for getting this new couple together. But there was no need to worry, because someone else was proud as could be to call himself matchmaker.

"Looks like I made a love connection!" Aleck bragged in Woodshop.

"Yes. Thanks to you, I'm getting up close and personal views of Mouth's..." Ack. "Mouth."

Mouth had memorized Manda's schedule and found time to sneak quick kisses before and after every class. I don't think I need to remind you how much this grosses me out. My position on public displays of affection is pretty straightforward. To me, PDA stands for: PLEASE. DON'T. ACK.

"'Mouth' is a weird word, isn't it?" Aleck said, obviously changing the subject but not really. "The more you say it, the weirder it sounds. Mouth. Mouth. Mouth."

I should have been relieved that Aleck was talking to me at all, considering how rudely I dismissed him on Saturday night. But he hadn't even given me an opportunity to apologize before annoying me all over again.

"Why don't you keep your 'mouth mouth mouth' shut for a while?" I said, deliberately taking a stool as far away from Aleck as possible.

This would prove to be a pointless gesture.

"You've all made tremendous progress over the last six weeks," Mr. Pudel announced to the room. He grandly swept his hands toward our gallery of birdhouses, napkin holders, and spoons. "It's time to take it to the next level."

"Ooh! Ooh!" shouted out Aleck. "Sporks?"

"No, not sporks," Mr. Pudel replied genially.

"Sporks must be the next *next* level," Aleck said in a loud whisper to Mouth, who had just slipped into the classroom five minutes late.

"You could all benefit from learning the art of cooperation," Mr. Pudel said. "Your next assignment will be a collaboration between you and a partner."

Around the room, alliances were already being made. Mouth and Aleck bumped fists.

"Dude, we're a team."

As the Only Girl in the Room, there was a moment there when I thought I might be lucky enough to be the odd one out. I'd get to work on the project all by myself! That positive thinking lasted until Mr. Pudel completed his thought.

"A partner *of my choosing*," he said with special emphasis.

Everyone groaned. Teachers love pairing up students instead of letting us exercise our right to choose partners for ourselves. It always goes terribly. Teachers inevitably mess with the delicate social order by pairing up Hots with Nots or ex-boyfriends with ex-girlfriends or crushers with crushees. Either they're totally clueless, or they love creating drama. I haven't figured out which.

Anyway, in accordance with the Inevitable Laws of Terrible Teacher Partnering, there were many boys in the class who would make bad partners for me, but only one person who qualified as the worst. And that's precisely who I got.

"Aleck and Clem," Mr. Pudel shouted.

Of course.

After naming the other pairs, Mr. Pudel continued, "You can design and make anything you want, but you have to work together."

We all just sat there, awaiting further instructions. Apparently there were no further instructions.

"Now get to work!" Mr. Pudel commanded.

Everyone scurried around the room, switching up their seating arrangements to work with their new partners. Aleck thumbs-upped merrily from across the room, showing off his bloodred half manicure from my PARTY!!! I charged at him as if I were a bull and he a cape-waving matador.

"Why does this keep happening to me?" I asked.

"What?"

"This!" I said, circling my hands wildly in the air between us.

"By 'this,'" Aleck said, mimicking my out-of-control gesture, "do you really mean me? Why do *I* keep happening to you?"

Why did Aleck keep happening to me?

Ack.

When Aleck says things like that, I understand why Manda and Sara call him a weirdo. I mean, who says things like that?

Aleck does.

Yes. Aleck is weird for sure, but that's what makes him interesting. And he's also consistently kinder to me than any of my other friends. This boy/girl stuff is so confusing. Why is it socially acceptable for Manda to make out with Mouth but totally uncool for me and Aleck to be just friends?

But I couldn't say any of that, of course. Who says things like that?

Besides Aleck, that is.

So this is what I said instead: "I'M NOT EVEN SUP-POSED TO BE IN THIS CLASS."

Aleck took a step back and gave me a measured look.

"But you *are* in this class," Aleck said. "And I *am* your partner on this project."

"So?"

"So let's make the most of it," he said. "Let's make something awesome."

He extended his fist. Part of me wanted to punch him. The other part of me knew it was pointless to resist. So I bumped knuckles right back. I consider this gesture to be my unspoken apology for my slumber-party rant, and Aleck's grin his silent acceptance.

Chapter Eighteen

Hooray for cross-country practice! The only guaranteed drama-free part of my day!

Until today.

OF COURSE.

"You tired, Notso?" Shandi asked during our warm-up stretches.

"Not especially," I said as I reached for my toes. "Do I look tired?"

"You look like you had quite a weekend," Shauna said.

Uh-oh.

"Who knew you were such a rebel?" Shandi asked.

"It's a good thing you didn't invite us," Shauna said. "Attending parties thrown by criminal types like you could sully our fine reputation. . . ."

Wait.

WHAT?

Whoa.

The Sampson twins knew about what happened on Saturday night? I guess Hope really wasn't exaggerating when she said the whole school was gossiping about my PARTY!!! Even eighth-grade Hots!

"*Wickywickywhoopwhoopwickywicky.*"

Padma was beatboxing. Then she started rapping.

"*Notso, Notso, brains and innocence. Throws a party, gotta call the ambulance!*"

"I didn't call 911," I said, trying to set the record straight. "My sister drove Dori home...."

But Padma was on a roll.

"*Notso, Notso, sweet and eager to please. Throws a party, and gotta call the police.*"

Okay. I couldn't exactly dispute that one. Gladdie had called in a favor to her friends in the police department.

"Don't believe the hype," I said. "It was kinda boring."

"You know what I did on Saturday night?" Molly asked.

This got everyone's attention because Molly hardly ever talks.

"What?" we all asked.

"I can't remember." She paused. "Now *that's* boring."

And we all laughed and sprawled out on the gym floor

to stretch and laughed some more. The girls were all being jokey about it, but their message was clear: They all wished they had been a part of the infamous sleepover. Unlike everyone else who had expressed regret in not having been there, these were girls I actually knew and liked and should have invited. I'd been too caught up in my own paranoia about being excluded to see that I'd actually excluded them!

My teammates cheer for me in good races and bad. They congratulate me when I'm up and comfort me when I'm down. But it honestly had never occurred to me that Padma or Molly or especially the Sampson twins would want to be invited to a slumber party at my house. Even worse, it had never occurred to me to invite them. I felt like such a jerk.

Thankfully, the Sampson twins changed the subject.

"So, Halloween," said Shauna, twisting her hips to the left.

"We have a fantastic group-costume concept," said Shandi, twisting her hips to the right.

And then they exchanged supersecret twin smiles.

"The best part about it is…" Shauna began.

"The whole team can take part!" Shandi finished.

Padma and Molly stood upright from their lunges and eyed each other warily.

"You want us?" Padma asked.

"Heck yeah!" Shandi said. "It's really…"

She shot a quick look at me before zeroing in on her twin.

"A team effort!" they said together.

Padma and Molly pumped their fists into the air.

"Yesssssss!"

I touched my toes, avoided eye contact, and felt conflicted.

"Yo, Notso. Do you already have a costume planned?" Shandi asked.

Did I? I hadn't discussed the Chibi Girls—or the periodic table, for that matter—with Manda or anyone else since Saturday night.

"We thought it would be cool if the whole team did this together," Shauna continued. "It might encourage more girls to go out for the team next year."

"That would be cool," Molly said, which from her is, like, a ringing endorsement.

Even with a major social boost from the Sampson twins, I doubted very much that the cross-country team could be cool, you know, by the Manda-and-Sara definition of coolness. I don't know why I suddenly felt so pressured to live up to their narrow definition of coolness, but I did. So much so that I just couldn't commit to my teammates until I knew whether the periodic table was, um, off the table.

"Let me get back to you," I said, trying to make eye contact with all the girls. "Okay?"

The Sampson twins did their telepathic thing again.

"That's cool, no pressure," Shauna said.

"But it really won't be the same without you," Shandi said.

The Sampson twins seemed pretty blasé about my non-commitment, all "whatever" in the true sense of the word and not all sarcastic-like. But Padma's and Molly's faces fell.

"Oh, sure," Molly said with a hard tone I'd never heard before. "Why commit to us when you have so many other options?"

"No! That's not what I meant!"

Padma stiffened. "No, really. I should've known better. You're, like, popular now. Why do something with us when you've got so many other friends?"

How wrong they were! I wasn't popular. I was just a hot topic right now for my involvement in events that didn't even happen to me AND mostly didn't happen the way everyone thought they did. Sure, it's kind of flattering to be noticed. But that's not friendship. That's just gossip.

I wanted to tell them this. But all four girls had already taken off for the track. And even though I could have, I didn't try to catch up with them. I felt like they had every reason to leave me behind.

Chapter Nineteen

The post-PARTY!!! bounce in social status has had an unexpected consequence among my friends: a truce. That's right. The unimaginable has happened. For the rest of the week following the sleepover, Bridget and Dori joined us at the round table for lunch!

"There's no reason why we can't all be friends," Manda said on Day One of the Cafeteria Table Truce.

"Omigod! I totally agree," said Sara, making room for the other girls.

"Me too!" said Dori.

"Me three!" said Bridget.

And Hope flashed me a look that said, *"THIS WON'T END WELL."*

I've tried to be more optimistic, if only because it was

my sleepover—inspired by my sister's IT List—that brought us all together. Still, after a week of getting along at lunch and a girls-only weekend trip to the movies (the boyfriends all refused to watch *Girl Power 6: Super Chicks!*), I'm still skeptical that this alliance will last. I can't be sure if the Manda-Sara/Dori-Bridget truce is motivated by IT List #1: 1 BFF < 2 BFFs < 4 BFFs < 8 BFFs < INFINITY BFFs or IT List #2: Have fun with your enemies.

Hope thinks it's the latter.

"You really don't think Manda and Sara have had a change of heart about Dori and Bridget?" I whispered to Hope as she sat down next to me for the movie.

"No."

"Why not?"

Hope sighed and answered simply, "History."

The lights went down, and Hope didn't elaborate. To be honest, I don't want to know what happened in the past. I know ignorance isn't bliss. It's dangerous. There's a quotation on the wall of our Social Studies classroom that reads: "Those who don't study history are doomed to repeat it." But when it comes to these friendships, I can't help but feel I'm doomed if I do and doomed if I don't.

Do or don't *what*, you ask?

JUST ABOUT ANYTHING.

This is not a positive attitude to have about one's

friends. It's enough to make me want to spend every lunch period eating at Coach/Nurse Fleet's desk.

When Manda isn't making a bid for the Nobel Peace Prize, she and Mouth are still ACKING me out. Fortunately, there's not enough room for everyone's boyfriends at our lunch table, so I'm spared their PDAs while I'm trying to eat. On the upside, Manda and Mouth's make-outs are getting easier to avoid because they're on a schedule: before homeroom, before all eight periods, and before the buses roll out. It's like clockwork, which is why Hope and I turned Manda and Mouth's make-outs into a new unit for measuring time: the M3. There are ten M3s per school day.

It makes me feel better to know that there's someone else who is as immature about kissing and boyfriend/girlfriend stuff as I am.

"Mouth's periodic-table costume would be tungsten," I said to Hope as we passed the couple in the parking lot this morning, Day Eight of the Cafeteria Table Truce. "Get it? TONGUE-sten?"

"Ew! That's so gross!" Hope snorted with laughter. "But funny."

That joke reminded me that there were only forty M3s until Halloween. This sounds a lot longer than it is.

"So..." I said to Sara in homeroom. "We never settled on a group costume."

"We didn't?"

"No," I said. "We didn't."

She gave this some thought. "Omigod! Right! *We* didn't. You and I. Didn't."

"So...?" I asked.

"*We*—Manda and me and, um, everybody—don't want you to stress about the Chibi Girls. So go with nerdium if you still want to."

"Really?"

"Really!"

Whew! They had come around to my periodic-table idea after all! It would have been nice if they had thought to tell me sooner, but I wasn't about to get all hung up on those details. I was just relieved to feel like I was sort of a part of the group again. And there were plenty of elements to choose from, so I could invite the Sampson twins and Padma and Molly to be a part of the periodic table, too!

For the rest of the day I looked forward to settling the matter at cross-country practice. I'd felt kind of awkward around them lately, ever since they accused me of—gasp!—POPULARITY.

"Hey, Shauna, Shandi, Padma, Molly," I said when I saw them in the locker room. "So I checked with my friends, and I'm totally free to do a group costume with you! And I've got a pretty great idea...."

The Sampson twins, Padma, and Molly exchanged looks.

"Gee, thanks," Padma said, not sounding thankful at all. "But Shauna and Shandi's idea is awesome, so we're doing that. We're covered."

"Oh."

I'd hoped I'd at least have a chance to argue for my costume. But that wasn't happening.

"Sorry!" Molly said, not sounding sorry at all.

Padma and Molly slammed their lockers shut and headed out to the track. The Sampson twins lingered.

"No one likes feeling like a half friend," Shauna said.

Shandi just nodded solemnly. Her sister had said it all.

It's hard to believe the Sampson twins are only a year older than I am. They're already at, like, Gladdie levels of wisdom. For the rest of practice I thought about Shauna's words. After twelve sad laps, here's what I figured out:

Half friendships are all I have!

Bridget is my friend when Dori isn't around. Dori is my friend when Bridget makes her. Sara is my friend when she wants to spread intel or get ammo. Manda is my friend when she wants someone to boss around. And Hope? Well, she's a tricky one. We're kind of having another friendship breakthrough right now. ("Only fifteen hundred more M3s until we graduate from junior high!" she said cheerfully after Mr. Odd's particularly snoozy Physical Science lecture today.) But I'm kind of paranoid that I'm just setting myself up for disappointment. I guess I haven't really gotten over how she froze me out at my own sleepover. What's to stop her from ditching me for Manda and Sara again? Maybe winning the prize for best group costume could be just the thing to bring us all together. But would winning wreck my chances at developing deeper friendships with my teammates?

Ack.

Finally, as anyone could have predicted, my partnership with Aleck is turning out to be less of a collaboration and more of a battle for/against crazy.

Here are my ideas for our Cooperative Woodshop Project:

1. A box.
2. A yo-yo.
3. A holiday ornament.

Okay. I admit it's not the most creative list. But if we had chosen any of the above, we'd be finished by now.

Here are Aleck's ideas for our Cooperative Woodshop Project:

1. A hot-air balloon.
2. A break-dancing robot.
3. A double-necked electric guitar.

Every day we argue over the impossibility of these projects.

"We cannot build a hot-air balloon out of balsa wood."

"If Reese's had that attitude, we wouldn't have the peanut-butter cup."

AND SO ON.

At this rate, we're never going to finish our project. WHATEVER IT IS.

Ugh. The only lesson the group Halloween-costume drama and my Cooperative Woodshop Project have taught me is this: Sometimes it's so much easier to work alone.

Chapter Twenty

Trick or treat?

This Halloween was a whole bunch of both.

If you recall, I'd told Manda, Sara, Bridget, Dori, and Hope at the PARTY!!! how simple it would be to make their periodic-table costumes: black leggings and white T-shirts with the letter symbols for their elements. After debating my various options, I'd decided to go with lead after all. I did this as a gesture of goodwill. You know, to prove to my friends that I could take a joke and it was possible to put all pettiness behind us and that there were no hard feelings from the PARTY!!!

HA!

Since the periodic-table group costume was my stroke of brilliance, I assumed they'd follow my directions. So imagine my surprise when I showed up at the bus stop in my Pb tee to find Bridget wearing a neon pink wig, pounds of makeup, and a tangerine T-shirt with a turquoise letter *H* for hydrogen. Okay. I'm not going to lie. I was a little bit annoyed that she hadn't listened to me. But I quickly decided to take the high road because I know how much Bridget loves to dress up and I was still so flattered that they'd all agreed to go with my idea instead of Manda's.

"Oh, wow!" I enthused. "I love your, um, *unique* interpretation of the theme!"

"Gee, thanks, Jess," she said shyly. "That's, like, really cool of you to say so."

Bridget fiddled with her pink bangs.

"I guess I thought we'd all try to look the same," I said. "You know, as I'd carefully instructed."

"Ohhhh…yeah…" Bridget said vaguely. "YAY! The bus!"

And this brought the discussion to a close. As it always does.

When I got off the bus, Dori and Scotty weren't in their usual spot. I didn't think anything of it, because Hope had caught my attention from all the way across the parking lot. I couldn't miss her. She was wearing platform sneakers and had styled her hair into a high top-of-the-head ponytail that made her about ten feet tall. Even at a distance I could see the hot-pink letter *B* on her shirt.

BORON? Really? Of all the elements to pick from? What a quirky choice for a quirky girl. That's what I was thinking when I saw Manda and Sara pushing their way through crowds of zombies, vampires, and werewolves to catch up to her. Manda had a letter *C* stretched across her impressive chest. Sara had an *I* on hers. Carbon. Okay. It made perfect sense that Manda saw herself as an essential element found in all life-forms. But iodine? Why would Sara pick iodine...?

As I approached the group, I heard them break out into a familiar tune.

"Giggle giggle giggle POP!
HA-ha-HA-ha-HA-ha-HA!"

Did you figure it out before I did?

Manda wasn't carbon.

Bridget wasn't hydrogen.

Sara wasn't iodine.

Hope wasn't boron.

MY FRIENDS HAD GONE CHIBI WITHOUT ME.

Okay. So I never wanted to Chibi in the first place. But that's not the point! The point is that these girls who are supposed to be my friends INTENTIONALLY MIS-LED me.

Correction: They intentionally MISS LEAD me.

Get it?

BECAUSE I WAS THE FOOL DRESSED AS LEAD.

Har dee har har.

According to my sister's IT List, there's no *I* in *clique.* But there are two *Is* in *Chibi.* And even though I should have put it all together at that point, I nearly fell over when I saw for myself who they had picked to be the second *I* instead of me.

"I'm so, so, so sorry I'm late!" Dori apologized. "I missed the bus because it took me forever to put on these fake eyelashes!"

Two weeks ago, Manda/Sara and Bridget/Dori loved sharing with me how much they couldn't stand each other. And now they were besties and I was the one on the outs? I TOTALLY LOST IT. Which is ironic because lead is known for being a very stable element and HOLY COW EVEN IN A CRISIS MY NERD SELF ALWAYS WINS OUT OVER MY TRYING-TO-BE-NORMAL SELF.

"You…you…" I spluttered. "I…I…"

That's about all I could get out of my furious mouth.

Only Hope acknowledged my left-outness.

"I thought you knew," she said. "I swear."

"Well, I didn't."

"They told me you knew we were going to be the Chibis

and you didn't care because you were going ahead with your periodic-table idea anyway and..."

The more Hope talked, the madder I got.

"SHUT IT UP, SHUTTY!"

This made no sense, of course. I was too angry to make any sense.

So I stormed off before I could say more stupid things and Hope could make more excuses I wasn't in the mood to hear. The other girls didn't notice my exit because they were too busy being showered with attention. Everyone wanted them to sing "Giggle Pop" on command. And they were only too happy to comply.

"Giggle giggle giggle POP!
HA-ha-HA-ha-HA-ha-HA!"

Every *"HA-ha-HA-ha-HA-ha-HA!"* was a dagger to the heart.

To make matters worse, without any other elements to back me up, my costume made NO SENSE AT ALL. I should have been heading to homeroom, but I was on my way to the locker room to grab a spare T-shirt I could change into. I wasn't where I was supposed to be, which is how I ended up right in Aleck's path. In a hallway filled with superheroes and video-game villains, he, like me, was wearing a plain white T-shirt with black lettering. Only his said simply: COSTUME.

"Hey, Clem!"

He looked right down at my chest, which would have been pervy and inappropriate if there was anything worth looking at down there.

"Pb," he said.

"Uh-huh."

He scratched his head, and his hand went deep into the tangle of his hair.

"Peanut butter?" he guessed.

I walked away without correcting him. He called out after me.

"Where's the jelly?"

Winners of the school-wide costume contest got a fifty-dollar gift card to a bookstore. This was annoying because I was the only one—okay, besides Hope, maybe— who would've spent the prize money on reading material instead of whipped-creamy cocoa and cupcakes at the in-store café that they would later moan and groan about eating because calories and fat and UGH.

The Chibi Girls were shoo-ins.

That is, until the Pineville Junior High girls' cross-country team arrived on the Halloween scene. I heard the laughter before I saw them.

"Best! Group! Costume! Ever!"

And it was. It really and truly was.

Shandi and Shauna were dressed as different birds. Padma wore a bear costume. And Molly looked hilariously tiny but tough in an oversize PJHS Football uniform. I almost keeled over. My teammates had dressed up as Mighty the Seagull's Last Dance!

"We usually have our costumes planned out six months in advance," said Shandi, decked out in a less elaborate version of the red-white-and-blue-feathered costume I had worn during my secret stint as the school mascot.

"But we didn't come up with this one until last month," said Shauna, who wore a much-larger-than-life version of the lovesick goose who had chased me all over the field.

"My friends in North Dakota will never believe this," said Padma, dressed as our rival school's mascot, who had also chased me all over the field.

Molly's helmet dipped below the black lines smudged under both eyes.

"Sorry we didn't include you."

This time she actually sounded apologetic.

"It's okay," I said.

It really was okay. It was oddly satisfying to know I'd inspired my teammates—even if they didn't know it. Part of me wanted to tell them that I had been the mascot. But I held back. Not because I didn't trust them to keep my former secret identity a secret—because honestly, all that had happened way, way back in September, which felt like a bazillion years ago and hardly needed to stay a secret anymore—but because I didn't want them to think I was somehow trying to take credit for their idea. They had come up with something *hilarious* and *genius* and *school spirited*, which is exactly the sort of thing that wins over vice principals judging costume contests. This was my teammates'—my friends'—moment. I was happy enough to watch them enjoy themselves.

AND OKAY, I WAS ALSO HAPPY THAT THEY BEAT OUT THE CHIBI GIRLS.

I didn't see my teammates again until practice. By the time I got there, they were already out of their costumes and in their gym clothes. After a conspiratorial huddle, the foursome approached me at my locker.

"Here's your share of the winnings," Shandi said, holding out a ten-dollar bookstore gift card.

I eyed the prize but didn't reach for it.

"C'mon. It's easier to divide fifty dollars by five instead of four," Shauna coaxed.

"But I didn't do anything!"

"If it wasn't for your performance on that field," Shandi said, "we would've never come up with this idea."

Wait. What? Whoa.

Were they telling me what I thought they were telling

161

me? Shandi and Shauna exchanged not-so-secret twin smiles that said yes.

"Did Coach Fleet tell you?" I asked.

Coach Fleet had nursed my injuries after the goose and the bear and two football teams had chased me beak-first into the goalpost.

"Nope," Shandi said. "Shauna and I figured it out when we saw you run for the first time at practice."

"You did?" I asked in disbelief.

"We pointed it out to Paddy and Mols when we told them we were splitting the prize and they were like…"

"NO DUH!" shouted Padma and Molly.

"Really?" I still couldn't quite believe it. "How?"

"When you run," Shauna explained, "you flail your arms across your body in the same exact way the seagull flapped its wings."

"I do?" I asked, incredulous that they had noticed such a thing and never mentioned it before. "I did?"

My teammates nodded vigorously.

"You're wasting a lot of energy that way," Shauna added. "You could take a few more seconds off your time if you corrected your body mechanics."

"Too bad the season's almost over," said Molly.

"Wickywickywhoopwhoopwickywicky," beatboxed Padma before launching into a spontaneous verse.

"Shauna, Shandi, Padma, Molly, and JD. Friends like family, Pineville Girls' X-C!"

And as corny as it was, we all joined in on the chant. I swear our five voices shouted louder than the CHEER TEAM!!! and Spirit Squad combined.

"Shauna, Shandi, Padma, Molly, and JD. Friends like family, Pineville Girls' X-C!"

There's only another week left before the Sampson twins move on to the basketball team. Padma is trying out for the school musical. Molly hopes to be the first girl to qualify for the micro weight class on the wrestling team. I don't know what I'm going to do this winter. We all promise to run track in the spring, but that team draws a much larger turnout than cross-country. We'll be five of many.

I'll miss just the five of us.

I'll miss the sound of the beads in the Sampson twins' braids click-clacking with every bounce in their step. I'll miss the determined bulldog face Molly wears whenever she sprints up Killer Hill. I'll even miss Padma's terrible rhymes.

I'll miss seeing these girls at practice after school every day.

I'm so glad I came to appreciate them before I missed out on their friendships altogether. If only the Chibi Girls would come to a similar epiphany about me.

Chapter Twenty-One

I arrived home in a mixed-up mood.

On the upside: I was happy with my X-C friends.

On the downside: I didn't have much time left to spend with them.

On the way downside: I wasn't happy with my G&T friends.

On the waaaaaay downside: I had *too much* time left to spend with them.

Okay. So I was definitely more down than up. I wanted someone to sort it out for me. And that person just happened to be at the house looking for the finishing touches on her own Halloween costume.

"I need to find my black leather motorcycle jacket," Bethany said. "Rodger and I are going as Danny and Sandy from *Grease*."

"You're still seeing Rodney?" I asked.

"Rodger," she corrected. "And yes!" She triumphantly pulled a hanger out of her massive closet. "We're seeing each other."

"You and the neighborhood nerd?"

"Jessie!" Bethany snapped. "That isn't very nice!"

Bridget and Burke. Dori and Scotty. Manda and Mouth. And now Bethany and Rodger-not-Rodney. None of them makes any sense to me. Will I ever get how boyfriend/girlfriend stuff happens?

"He's not your type at all."

"Shhh! He'll hear you! He's just down the hall in the office!"

"Managing Mom and Dad's flow of communication?" I asked pointedly. "You can't keep your expulsion a secret forever."

"I don't have to keep it a secret forever! Just until I've worked everything out. But enough about me!" Bethany said, slipping into the leather jacket and admiring its perfect fit in the full-length mirror. "Let's talk about you! What's going on with your friends from the PARTY!!!?"

"Oh, everything's perfect," I said, taking a seat on the floor. "They're all besties, and I'm on the outside looking in."

My sister, still looking at herself in the mirror, pursed her lips and sighed. "Did you follow the IT List?"

"I sure did!" I replied with fake cheer. "Total fails on numbers one through three! But that's okay, right? 'When all else fails: CANDY.' Right? Wrong! Are you kidding? When I offered them candy, they all freaked out, but they're totally fine with trick-or-treating as the Chibi Girls, which doesn't make any sense—"

"Wait." My sister interrupted my rant. "You offered them what?"

"Candy," I said. "Like number four on the IT List said to. So Gladdie and I made chocolates that I brought to school and a bunch of sweets for the sleepover and..."

Bethany sighed and shook her head like, "Nonononono."

"They thought you were trying to make them fat, didn't they?"

I nodded.

"And pimply?"

I nodded.

"I would've thought the same thing," Bethany said. "Like you were trying to sabotage me...."

Now I was totally, totally confused.

"But what about 'When all else fails: CANDY'?"

"Candy is a person," Bethany said.

"What?"

"An old lady in the neighborhood who babysat me sometimes," Bethany said. "Back in the sixties she had an advice column in *Ladies First* magazine. She'd seen and heard it all. Nothing shocked her. And she was totally objective. She'd tell it to you straight because she had nothing to win or lose."

I remembered what Sara had said: *Everything is always a competition.*

"That's exactly what I need! An objective opinion from someone who has nothing at stake! Can I talk to her?"

"No," Bethany said.

"No?"

"No," Bethany repeated. "Because she's dead."

"Jeez! That's depressing!"

"Not really," said Bethany. "She was waaaaay old. She lived a full life."

So. Let's summarize. When all else failed—which it HAD—my sister had encouraged me to seek advice from someone who is very inconveniently DEAD. Bethany isn't known for being practical, but COME ON.

"Thanks for the totally worthless advice," I said, standing up to leave.

Bethany sighed and patted me on the head. She does this whenever she wants to remind me that she's the big sister here, even if we're the same height.

"She's not the only wise old lady around here, you know," Bethany said.

And then she made her grand exit, as she has a knack for doing.

Duh.

DUH. DUH. DUH.

My sister was right. I didn't have Candy. But I did have another wise old lady I could turn to for guidance. And it seemed like she was already waiting for me in the kitchen when I arrived.

"How's it going, gorgeous?" asked Gladdie as she stirred a pot on the stove.

I remembered Gladdie's advice: *Be direct! Say what you need to say!*

"All my friends are friends with each other," I said. "But I don't feel like I fit in with any of them anymore. Or maybe I do. I don't know."

I'm not sure what Bethany meant by IT List #5: There is no *I* in CLIQUE. But I'm pretty sure it wasn't a command to exclude myself from all my friends, even though that's exactly what seems to be happening.

"How long has this been going on?" Gladdie asked.

"Since the sleepover."

"That's not very long," she said.

"It feels like forever."

"That's because you're young."

She stopped stirring and looked me right in the eyes.

"Friendships change because people change. Stop trying to make them into something they're not."

"Friendships? Or people?"

"Both." She broke into a bright-red-lipsticked smile. "Let people—and friendships—be what they're meant to be."

I nodded. I think I understood what she was getting at, but I wanted to make sure.

"Even if I realize that a friendship isn't meant to be at all?" I asked.

My grandmother was still smiling at me, but her gaze softened, shifting her expression into something slightly sadder than before.

"Especially then," she said. "No friend is perfect. Even the tightest of bonds are tested now and again. But a true friend makes you feel more good than bad."

I let these words sink in. There really wasn't anything I could add to improve upon what she'd just said. I sniffed the air.

"Tomato-basil soup?" I asked hopefully.

"What else with my three-cheese panini!"

Mmmmmmm. Comfort food. In every sense of the word. My grandmother was ready to provide me with just what I needed—and I hadn't even asked for it. Right then, I realized that kind of intuitive being-there-ness was missing in all my friendships. My attempts at making those connections are hit-or-miss. I used to have a bond like that with Bridget. At times I think I could have it with Hope or the girls on the cross-country team. And yes, when Manda entrusts me with her Saturday night, or Sara confides in me, I feel like there's potential there, too. I guess only time will tell which bonds will stick.

One thing I know for sure: The connection between Gladdie and me is unbreakable and unfakeable. I just wish I felt the same way about my friends.

I rushed over to hug her. My show of gratitude must have caught Gladdie by surprise because she almost fumbled her ladle into the pot.

"Thank you!" I said. "For everything."

"You are always welcome, Jessie." She gripped me tighter. "For everything."

I inhaled deeply once more. The soup smelled soooooo goooooood. My mouth was watering.

And yes, maybe my eyes were a little bit, too.

Chapter Twenty-Two

On Monday we all went back to school in our normal clothes, and Manda/Sara and Dori/Bridget acted all normal around me as if it were a totally normal day and they hadn't, like, totally excluded me on Halloween.

"You didn't want to be a Chibi," Manda said.

"Omigod! It's so true," Sara added. "When I told you to go with nerdium, you were totally okay with it."

"If anything," Manda said, "*you* rejected *us*."

I thought about what Gladdie had said: *Friendships change because people change. No friend is perfect. Even the tightest of bonds are tested now and again. But a true friend makes you feel more good than bad.*

After a few breaths, I was able to see how Manda and Sara might have a point: I *had not* wanted to be a Chibi.

I *had* rejected them. Still, they purposely tricked me into thinking we were in on the periodic table together. I had no idea that my decision to "go with nerdium" meant I'd be going it ALONE.

"It's not like it matters, because we lost," Dori said sourly.

"To that crazy chicken," Bridget said with a quick wink for just me that said "Don't worry; I won't tell."

"Seagull," mouthed Hope, also for my benefit.

"Yeah, well, maybe if your false eyelashes hadn't fallen off, we would've won!" Manda griped to Dori.

"Omigod!" Sara groaned. "They were like giant tarantulas crawling across your cheeks!"

"Really?" Dori shot back. "You didn't even try to apply Bouncy's face tattoo!"

The days of the Cafeteria Table Truce were numbered. And judging from the mix of annoyance and amusement on Hope's face as she watched the girls bicker, I wasn't the only one who knew it.

"I told you this wouldn't end well."

Part of me wanted to congratulate Hope on her all-knowingness. But the other part of me was still sort of annoyed at her for whatever role she played in the Chibi Girl deception. Plus, it wasn't a prediction worthy of celebration, because neither one of us had wanted it to come true. So I just sort of nodded, which seemed to disappoint her, but I didn't give it much thought because the eighth-period bell finally rang and the whole squabbling lunch bunch headed for Home Ec with Hope trailing behind. Their departure brought my reluctant participation in the friendship drama to an end for the day. That—*HOORAY!!!*—was something worth cheering about.

How could I have known a whole new dimension of drama was about to begin?

Chapter Twenty-Three

With time running out and my stellar academic record in jeopardy, Aleck and I had finally settled on a much simpler idea for our Cooperative Woodshop Project, one that seemed sort of doable when compared with impossible projects that defied the laws of physics and sensible thinking:

A footstool.

Unfortunately, not doable enough. Considering our last project was a birdhouse, making a piece of furniture meant to be used by actual human beings was pretty ambitious. And no matter how hard we tried or how much research we did on the making of footstools, our construction was wobblier than a bad game of Jenga. Aleck and I were down to eleven M3s before our project was due. That's one class and one day, if you aren't keeping track. It wasn't looking very good.

"Our footstool is going to fall apart!" I said, pointing out the obvious. "It's due tomorrow! We'll fail!"

"We won't fail," Aleck insisted.

"So says the boy who got an F plus on his epic toothpick."

Aleck took a step back and looked at the wiggly wooden thing that was supposed to be our project.

"Maybe we're approaching this the wrong way."

"We're obviously approaching this the wrong way. Our footstool is on the verge of collapsing, and that's why we are going to f—"

Aleck let out a little whoop.

"THAT'S THE ANSWER," Aleck cried out, snapping his fingers. His fingernails, I might add, were still coated in red polish from my PARTY!!!

"What's the answer?"

"It's a collapsible footstool." He paused. "Get it?"

I definitely did not get it.

"We have to stop trying to make it into something it's not!" Aleck was getting excited now. "Let it be what it's supposed to be!"

This sounded familiar. But I couldn't place where I'd heard it before—or from whom—because I was too irritated by the sight of Aleck literally patting himself on the back.

"That's deep," he said, marveling at his own wisdom.

"That's dumb," I said.

"I'm deep," he said.

"You're demented."

"I am," Aleck said, unbowed by my lack of enthusiasm, "a misunderstood philosopher genius."

"Who is failing Woodshop and taking me down with him!" I shouted.

I was so frustrated that I had to leave the room. I found refuge in the girls' bathroom, which is the cleanest girls' bathroom in the entire school because no girls ever use it because NO GIRLS TAKE WOODSHOP. The downside to the cleanliness is that there isn't any interesting graffiti to decipher. I hadn't thought to bring along any reading material, so after roughly five minutes of examining the pores in my nose, I was pretty bored and decided to return to class to face off with my demented partner. The hall outside Woodshop is generally pretty deserted, so I wasn't looking out for oncoming foot traffic when—*CRASH!*

"Hey, now! I'm the defensive tackle, not you!"

It was Scotty, of all people. I'd rammed my head right into his shoulder.

"Oops! Sorry!" I said, rubbing my forehead. "I obviously wasn't paying attention."

"It's cool," Scotty said.

To tell the truth, I'd been going out of my way to avoid

him. Dori seemed more secure in their relationship since the Near-Death Experience at my PARTY!!! but I didn't want to take any chances.

So I said, "Um, okay. Cool." Pause. "See ya."

When I took a step toward the Woodshop classroom, he blocked my path.

Then he put on a frowny face.

"I should be mad at you."

I knew he wasn't referring to causing injury to his shoulder. Oh no! Did he still think I had something to do with spreading the old rumors about us? I was about to tell him how I thought he and Dori were a great couple and that I'd never stand in the way of their relationship and how I was as annoyed by all the gossip as he was—if not more—when he stunned me into silence.

"I can't break up with Dori," Scotty said, "and it's all your fault."

"WHAT?"

My shout echoed in the empty hallway. I dropped my voice to a whisper. "You're breaking up with Dori?"

He sighed and stuffed his hands deep into the pockets of his cargo pants.

"I want to, but I can't because of her near-death experience at *your* party," he said. "Only a jerk would break up with a girl right after a near-death experience, right?"

He was right. That would be a pretty jerky thing to do. And Scotty isn't a jerk. He's sweet. A little bit boring, maybe, but sweet. And when she isn't hating me, that describes Dori pretty well, too.

"You two really seem like a good match," I said. "Why do you want to break up with her, anyway?"

"Well," he said, looking down at his sneakers. "It's not fair to keep it going with Dori when I have feelings for another girl."

He lifted his head and looked me right in the eyes. And even though I'm totally clueless about boyfriend/girlfriend business, there was suddenly no question in my mind what girl he was referring to.

ME. HE WAS REFERRING TO ME. THE GIRL HE HAD FEELINGS FOR WAS ME ME ME—HOLY COW—ME.

And then, maybe sensing my usual cluelessness about boyfriend/girlfriend business, Scotty felt the need to be specific even though I really, really would have preferred if he hadn't.

"I mean, Dori's fine." He meant it in the same "okay, I guess" way I did when I used that word to describe him. "But you're legendary. You're Mighty the Seagull!"

SCOTTY KNEW, TOO. WAS THERE ANYONE WHO DIDN'T KNOW?

"H-how did you figure it out?" I asked.

A dreamy look crossed his face.

"I saw you at your locker after the pep rally," he said. "You had the tiniest red feather stuck in your hair. That's when I knew. I knew it was you."

"I did?" I asked. "You did?"

"No one else would've noticed," he said with a shy smile, "unless he was already looking."

Without another word he hurried off, leaving me alone with his confession: Scotty had noticed me.

Me?

Yes.

Me.

Dazed, I turned back toward my classroom and caught Aleck ducking back inside. How long had he been hovering in the doorway?

And how much had he heard?

"So...Aleck..." I began sheepishly upon my return to Woodshop. "I..."

He held up his hands to shush me.

"Behold!"

He gestured grandly toward our Jenga footstool. It was, at the moment, standing upright like a footstool should.

"So?"

"Watch."

Then he reached underneath and folded the legs, and the footstool flattened to the floor.

"It's a collapsible footstool," Aleck said proudly. "Just like I said it was."

Then, just to prove it worked, he restraightened the legs, set it up, and propped his foot on top like he had survived a climb to the summit of Mount Everest.

"Ta-da!"

Aleck did it! He saved our project! I was sufficiently impressed to temporarily put aside what had just happened in the hallway with Scotty.

"You fixed it?" I asked. "In ten minutes?"

"Hinges! It was easy, Clem!" He was smiling broadly now. "We just had to let it be what it was supposed to be."

Where had I heard that before...?

Let people—and friendships—be what they're meant to be.

Gladdie.

The bell rang, and Aleck bolted out the door before I had a chance to tell him that maybe, just maybe, he was a genius after all.

Chapter Twenty-Four

I couldn't wait to tell Gladdie how funny it was to hear her advice come out of Aleck's mouth and what a weird coincidence that was. I also thought she might be able to help me sort out the latest development in The Scotty Scandal. But when I got home, her car was in the driveway with the trunk open. It was loaded up with her suitcases, her baking pans, and her knitting.

I looked for her inside.

"Hello?"

The kitchen was immaculate and not in use. I found her in the guest room, fluffing the pillows on the bed.

"You're leaving?" I asked. "Right now?"

"Afraid so, my loveliness," she said. "I gotta skedaddle. The Golden Mermaids got a gig doing the halftime show at the Senior Swimlympics."

Gladdie couldn't leave now! She had to help me sort out this business with Scotty!

"I need you here," I said all in a rush. "Or. Um. I mean, Mom and Dad think I do."

I don't know why—with my grandmother, of all people—I tried to put up a grown-up front.

"I told your parents that you're doing just fine," she said. "All twelve-year-olds should be as together as you are. Heck! You're more mature than some eighty-year-olds I know! You wouldn't believe some of the silliness that goes down at the Senior Center. I've got this friend Verna who—"

The phone rang, cutting off her juicy story about Verna. Gladdie gave me a nod that said "Go ahead and pick it up." So I did.

"Hey, it's me, Hope."

I recognized her voice, but I kind of understand why she felt the need to clarify. She had never called me before.

"Um, Hope?" Then to Gladdie. "It's my friend Hope."

"The one with the spectacular crimson curls," Gladdie marveled. "What I wouldn't do for a head of hair like that one."

"Yes," I confirmed. Then back to Hope. "Can I talk to you later because I'm saying good—"

Gladdie shooed away such nonsense.

"You and me, doll, we don't say good-bye," she said.

Then Gladdie gestured for me to bend down, so she could kiss the top of my head. I couldn't see it, but I imagined that she'd left behind a bright red lip print.

"Until next time," she said.

Then Gladdie curtsied and headed out the door without saying good-bye.

Until next time.

I apologized to Hope for making her wait.

"No, no, no!" she insisted. "I owe *you* an apology."

"For what?" I asked.

"For *what*? For being totally cuckoo lately!"

Normally, with any of my other friends, I'd feel obligated to say something like, *What? You? Cuckoo? No way*... but I actually respect Hope too much not to tell her the truth.

"Well," I said cautiously, "you have been a bit off for the past few weeks. But even on your worst day, you're still easier to deal with than other people we know."

Hope chuckled gratefully.

"You're being too nice."

She swallowed before continuing.

"Manda and Sara swore that you already knew that we were going ahead with the Chibi Girls. I should've known better than to believe them."

She paused again.

"But you believe me, right?"

I did believe her. Don't ask me why, but I did. And she wasn't done yet.

"And I know it hurt you when I was hanging out with Manda and Sara at your party. I didn't want to exclude you, but I felt like I didn't have a choice because Manda and Sara..."

In the millisecond between those words and the next, my overactive brain filled in the gap.

...are cooler, prettier, smarter, funnier, and better than you will ever be!

"...already got their periods."

Wait. WHAT? Whoa.

"So. Yeah. I got my period. For the first time."

"Congratulations! That's a big deal, right?"

I wouldn't know, because I haven't gotten mine yet.

"Yippee."

She didn't sound too psyched.

"It made me feel like *bleeeeeeech*. That's why I missed school those few days. That's why I was with Manda and Sara in the bathroom at your party. They gave me, um, supplies. And also tips on how I could make myself feel better...."

"They *did*?"

"You sound surprised."

"I am surprised," I confessed. "I mean, I wouldn't expect Manda and Sara to be so..."

"Helpful?"

Exactly.

Manda's thoughtfulness and Sara's discretion were totally unexpected. I'd have thought Manda would respond more along the lines of "Bleed it up, bleedy!" And I still can't believe Sara didn't blab, "Omigod! Hope is having her first period at the PARTY!!!" to anyone who'd listen. It sounds like they really came through for Hope. Right now I can't imagine them doing the same for me in that situation, but that doesn't mean they never will. Hope has been friends with them forever. I just met them two months ago. Maybe I simply haven't earned that level of loyalty from Manda and Sara yet.

But what if I never do?

"So that's why I left your party early," Hope went on, "and well, why I've been kind of all over the place. But it's over for now, I guess."

"Until NEXT month," I said ominously.

"Or who knows when? Manda and Sara told me that it's pretty irregular for the first few go-rounds and can take a while to stick to a regular cycle. So I'm pretty much on a twenty-four-seven period watch."

Part of me was so relieved to hear that Hope's moodiness was menstrual in origin and not caused by anything I had said or done. The other part of me was less excited than ever about the arrival of puberty with a capital *P*.

"Is it that uncomfortable?" I asked. "You know, when you get it?"

Hope took the question seriously. She thought about it for a few moments before coming up with the perfect description.

"It's worse than that stuffed feeling after eating one corn dog too many," she said. "But not as bad as eating an expired corn dog and barfing twelve hours straight."

"So it's, like, a five on the Corn Dog Scale of Period Discomfort," I said.

And we both laughed.

After we settled down, there was a beat or two of quiet. I was dying to tell someone about what had happened with Scotty in the hall, but I didn't know if now was the right time.

"Is there something you want to talk about?" Hope asked.

It's like she read my mind.

"Um, well, yes, actually."

"Speak up!" Hope urged. "Spit it out!"

If Gladdie had gotten to know her, she'd admire Hope for so much more than her red hair.

"I don't want to belittle the monumental importance of your inaugural menstrual cycle."

I don't know why the arrival of Hope's period inspired me to talk like a college professor. Hope snorted with laughter.

"So you're never going to tell me anything ever again because I got my period?"

"That doesn't make any sense, does it?" I said.

"No," she replied. "So spill it."

"So." I took a deep breath. "You remember all the rumors about me and Scotty?"

Hope put on a movie-preview voice-over baritone.

"THE SCOTTY SCANDAL."

"What if I were to tell you that Dori had a reason to be paranoid about me?"

"You like Scotty?" Hope gasped. "Like, *like* like Scotty?"

"Nooooooo!" I shrieked in protest. "But..."

I hesitated. At that point I could still sort of pretend that what had happened in the hallway had never happened. Only Scotty and I—and maybe Aleck?—knew otherwise.

"Are you going to tell me or what?" Hope asked eagerly.

I had to decide. Was Hope a friend, foe, or faux friend? Sharing this information with Hope was a risk, yes, but also an opportunity for our half friendship to become closer to whole.

"Listen up," I said. "I'll tell you everything."

And I did.

Chapter Twenty-Five

Hope and I talked for a long time. I didn't leave out any of the details of my conversation with Scotty, even the most embarrassing parts like how he had a thing for me in feathers.

"*You?*" Hope gasped. "You were the crazy chicken?"

"Seagull," I corrected.

I said it just like she always does, and for some reason this made us laugh longer and louder than it should have.

"You really didn't know it was me?" I asked. At this point I had assumed everyone had figured it out and was just waiting to spring that knowledge on me when I least expected it.

"No!" Hope insisted. "Although, now that I know the truth, some of those moves do seem familiar!"

"From where?" I asked.

"Like, when you bite into a grilled cheese sandwich and it's too hot and you start hopping up and down and flapping your hands in front of your face like it's going to help cool off your mouth. Very birdlike. But I only see the connection now that you've told me."

"You're the first person I've confessed to," I said. "Everyone else found out on their own."

"Well," Hope said, "your nonsecret is safe with me."

Despite all the motives I might have for not trusting any of my friends, I believed Hope when she said that.

Anyway, Hope is of the opinion that I should pretend the conversation with Scotty never happened. I'm not so sure I can pull off that lie because—apparently, in the eyes of Aleck and the Sampson twins and Scotty and whoever else sussed out my secret seagull identity—deception is not my strong suit. We might still be debating the pros and cons of this strategy if my sister hadn't knocked on my door.

"Sorry to interrupt," Bethany said after I ended the call. "But did Gladdie leave already?"

"Yeah," I said. "About a half hour, maybe an hour ago?"

The conversation with Hope had flowed so effortlessly that I'd lost track of time.

"Oh," my sister said, sounding deflated. "I'm sorry I missed her."

"Did you come here to say good-bye?"

"Well, yes," Bethany said, not convincingly.

I was skeptical of her motivations. Bethany rarely made an appearance at our house unless it was part of her ongoing mission to hide her college expulsion from my parents.

Bethany corrected herself.

"I mean no. I mean, Gladdie doesn't say good-bye. She says..."

"...Until next time," we said together.

My sister and I smiled to ourselves. And then Bethany surprised me by pushing my textbooks and T-shirts aside and making herself at home on my unmade bed. If I've spent roughly ninety minutes in my sister's bedroom over the past twelve years, she has spent approximately ninety seconds in mine.

"I wanted to thank her, too," she said. "If it weren't for her, I wouldn't be meeting with the dean next week to argue my case for being readmitted to school."

"You're what?"

"Gladdie encouraged me to pore over my old papers and exams to see if there was any chance that I'd been unfairly graded," she said. "Human error, you know."

Oh, if there is one thing I know well, it's human error.

"So Rodger went through my work and found an essay I'd written for my GOSSIP 301 final—"

"Wait," I interrupted her. "You failed a college class in gossip?"

"G-O-S-S-I-P."

I still didn't get it.

"Global Operative Success Strategies in Publicity," she explained. "And I didn't fail! That's the whole point! Rodger says my answer to a question about viral marketing campaigns was marked wrong, but it was totally right! And that answer was the difference between failing that class and passing, flunking out of school and being let back in!"

I was flabbergasted. Here I was all this time thinking that my sister was avoiding the issue, but she was actually facing it head-on. Maybe she wasn't as irresponsible as I thought. Perhaps she's not such a bad influence after all.

"Anyway, with me heading back to school and Mom and Dad finishing up their projects at work, everything should return to normal around here," Bethany continued. "It was the perfect time for Gladdie to get back to her own life."

At first I had resented the mere possibility that Gladdie had been dispatched to babysit me. But with my parents so crazy at work lately, it was nice having someone around to talk to. I can't remember the last time my parents and I said more than a "hello" or "good-bye" or "pass the ketchup" to one another. I know I should've been thrilled that they've been too distracted with their careers to be all up in my business.

But the truth is, I've actually kind of missed them. Of course I can never admit that out loud or else they'll NEVER LET ME OUT OF THEIR SIGHT FOR THE REST OF MY LIFE. So I kept my enthusiasm to an acceptable minimum.

"Good-bye, chocolate and cheese," I said. "Hello, kale casserole." I stuck out my tongue.

"Oh, I know!" Bethany agreed. "I swear I used to gain, like, a thousand pounds during Gladdie's visits. All those sweets!"

Trust me when I say my sister has always looked like a model for designer jeans.

She playfully pointed at my chest.

"But it looks like you haven't put on an inch!"

I followed her finger and looked down at the loose Pink Floyd T-shirt I was wearing. It had once been hers, bought to impress a rock-and-roll boyfriend. It would definitely fit my sister more...uh...snugly than me.

My sister was still giggling at her own joke.

Har dee har har.

"Oh, go ahead," I said. "Make fun of the only seventh grader who hasn't been visited by the Boob Fairy."

Bethany stopped laughing and nodded like she cared about my feelings.

"I'd assume that you haven't been visited by the Period Fairy, either," she said.

"From what I hear she's more like an elf with an attitude problem," I replied. "But no. I guess I'm a late bloomer."

"You're twelve! You're not a late bloomer!"

"I'll be thirteen in two months!" I shot back. "And I can't help but feel like a late bloomer when all my friends are already, like, full bouquets."

My sister laughed. But this time she was definitely laughing with me and not at me. She got up from my bed, walked over to my dresser, and inspected what limited beauty/hygiene products I had on display: deodorant, a hairbrush, a tangle of ponytail elastics, and a jar of Racy Red nail polish left over from the PARTY!!!

"I know exactly what you mean," my sister said, sniffing a never-worn bottle of too pink, too sweet perfume she'd given me last Christmas. She set the heart-shaped glass down delicately and turned to look me in the eyes. *"Exactly."*

I guess I was still thinking about the nail polish—and how it was the same color that was chipping off the finger-nails of Aleck's half-done hand—because I didn't immediately catch on to what my sister was trying to tell me.

"But maybe you've already outgrown my advice," she said. "Even if you haven't outgrown your training bra...."

It's a nonsupportive training bralette, thank you very much! But I didn't waste time explaining the difference.

"Are you saying what I think you're saying?" I said.

"I'm saying I couldn't fill out that T-shirt when I was your age, either."

"And?"

"I thought I was abnormal."

"Annnnnnd?"

"I'll do some digging and send it to you when I find it," my sister promised.

"Send what?"

I wanted to make sure we were talking about what I thought we were talking about. Making assumptions is how a person ends up dressing up for Halloween as the loneliest element on the periodic table and then doubly insulted by being mistaken for a jar of sandwich spread.

YOU KNOW. FOR EXAMPLE.

Bethany cleared her throat.

"The Guaranteed Guide to Stressing, Obsessing & Second-Guessing!"

"Yikes!"

"*Yikes!*" Bethany mocked my apprehension. "If that's your reaction, then maybe you're not ready for this list."

"I'm ready!" I insisted. "My brain is, like, totally, totally ready for this information! Even if my body isn't."

Okay. So I fibbed a little. If I'm being completely honest, I'm not sure if *any* part of me is prepared for what comes next.

Will I ever be?

Turn the page for a sneak peek!

Coming Soon

Chapter One

I know I'm not an early bloomer. But am I doomed to be a late bloomer? Or will I bloom sometime in between?

That's what I'm about to find out. Maybe. If I don't get too ACKED out.

I've never given much thought to my body. When I'm hungry, I eat. When I'm tired, I sleep. When I'm sick, I barf. That's the thing about bodies. When you're healthy and everything is functioning properly, your body is pretty easy to ignore. I mean, my body has been with me my entire life, and yet it barely crossed my mind because it just, you know, did the stuff bodies are supposed to do. My body makes me an excellent cross-country runner but a terrible gymnast. My body cannot execute a perfect aerial cartwheel but recovers quickly when an attempt to do so results in an epic face-smash in front of a gym full of bendy, twisty, perky CHEER TEAM!!! wannabes.

You know. For example.

I can't say for sure when my body changed things up. It started doing new stuff. Hard-to-ignore stuff. Like zits.

And my friends' bodies were also changing in noticeable—but different—ways. Like, on the last day of summer before the start of seventh grade, my (old?) best friend Bridget's body ALL OF A SUDDEN transformed from an ordinary sort of body into an extraordinary sort of body that got EVERYONE'S attention on the first day of school. Especially the boys'. Sometimes the changes are less obvious, like when I thought my (new?) best friend Hope was acting all cranky and crampy at a sleepover because she had a nasty stomach virus. She later revealed it was... well, not a virus at all. When she told me her first period was to blame for her bummerific crash on my couch, I was like, DUH.

As an A plus student, I should've known better. Actually, I *did* know better, and I have the perfect test scores to prove it! Last year, our sixth-grade teachers separated the girls from the boys and made us sit in different classrooms to watch The Movie. You know The Movie I'm talking about. It's The Movie about all the stuff that will happen to our bodies as we get older. Calling it THE Movie isn't entirely accurate, because there are actually two versions of The Movie. The girls watched The Movie all about girl stuff, and the boys watched The Movie all about boy stuff, which only *sort of* made sense to me. I mean, wouldn't it be beneficial for there to be just one Movie that covers girl stuff and boy stuff that we all watch together? So girls know what's really going on with boys? And vice versa? Maybe the boy version of The Movie unlocks the biggest mysteries about their behavior. If I had seen it, I might finally, finally, *finally* understand the unique male mind-body chemistry that makes all boys think farts are hilarious. But I didn't see it, so the best I can do is roll my eyes and pinch my nose every afternoon in Woodshop (THE CLASS I'M NOT SUPPOSED TO BE IN), where the boys outnumber the girls eleven (all of them) to one (me).

Rumor has it everyone watches an all-in-one version of The Movie next year in eighth grade. Until then, I guess I'm grateful that our teachers kept us apart. The girl version of The Movie was majorly cringe-worthy (*pee-yoo-ber-tee! men-stroo-ay-shun!*), and I still don't know if I'm capable of watching any version of The Movie in front of *actual boys*, because despite my stellar test scores and full schedule of Gifted & Talented classes, I am surprisingly childish about such things.

Or maybe it's more accurate to say UNsurprisingly

childish. My body isn't any closer to teenagerdom, so why should my brain be any different? Or my heart?

And that's why I'm afraid there's maybe something wrong with me. My body isn't responding the way a seventh-grade girl's body should. And I'm not just talking about the obvious physical stuff, like how I've gotten taller but the overall shape of my body has remained otherwise unchanged since first grade. Or how I'm the only one at my lunch table who hasn't gotten her period. I'm talking about, you know, the kind of boy/girl stuff that The Movie doesn't cover.

What kind of stuff? Here's an example:

Say there's a seventh-grade boy. He's smart. He's a football player. He's considered cute by the girls who consider such things. Boy has girlfriend. He wants to break up with her but can't because his girlfriend had a near-death experience at a sleepover—ahem, an EPIC sleepover—when she was poisoned by strawberry jelly. Only a jerk would initiate a breakup after a near-death experience, and this boy is no jerk. He's such a good boy that he knows it's not fair to keep things going with his girlfriend, because he has strong feelings for someone else—another girl. Other girl is an implausible object of affection because she could easily be mistaken for a very tall first grader.

OKAY. ENOUGH WITH THE HYPOTHETICALS.

Here's the real deal: Boy is Scotty. Girlfriend is Dori, my ex-BFF from elementary school. Her near-death-by-strawberry experience occurred at a sleepover at *my house*, so boy/Scotty blames *me* for not being allowed to break up with girlfriend/Dori so he can pursue his crush on other girl, who just happens to be—GUESS WHO?!?!—me. As other girl, I should be psyched, right? What seventh-grade girl wouldn't be? This is exactly the sort of juicy situation that turns a Not into a Hot. Being Scotty's girlfriend certainly worked to raise Dori's social profile. But here's the thing: I'm not interested in being Scotty's girlfriend and not only because the position is currently occupied by someone else. It's not Scotty's fault. He's ideal boyfriend material. I'm simply not interested in being his—or anyone else's—girlfriend.

AND THAT'S WHY I'M AFRAID SOMETHING IS WRONG WITH ME.

I watched The Movie. I aced the test afterward. So I know about hormones and how they're responsible for making everything in my body go KABOOM. Occasionally I'll come home from school in a grumpy mood for a legitimate reason, like after Aleck insisted we could make a hot-air balloon out of balsa wood for our Cooperative Woodshop Project, or when Manda and Sara bonked me repeatedly on the head with their inflatable Spirit Squad

Squeaky Sticks. Instead of acknowledging that these are valid reasons to be grumpy, my parents blame it on hormones and accuse me of "being hormonal" and complain about barely surviving the "hormonal years" the first time around with my sister a decade ago. But Mom and Dad are wrong. So, so, so wrong. Other than some attention-getting zits, there's zero evidence that my hormones are doing much of anything at all. And that's been perfectly fine with me.

Until big sis Bethany sent me another one of her IT Lists.

Sonya Sones

MEGAN McCAFFERTY is the *New York Times* bestselling author of the Jessica Darling series, *Bumped*, and *Thumped*. Her work has received honors from the American Library Association and the New York Public Library. She lives in Princeton, New Jersey, with her husband and son.

Her website is MeganMcCafferty.com.